ONCE UPON A TIME

STAFFORDSHIRE & WORCESTERSHIRE

Edited by Donna Samworth

First published in Great Britain in 2016 by:

 Young**Writers**

Remus House
Coltsfoot Drive
Peterborough
PE2 9BF
Telephone: 01733 890066
Website: www.youngwriters.co.uk
All Rights Reserved
Book Design by **ASHLEY JANSON**
© Copyright Contributors 2015
SB ISBN 978-1-78443-970-5

Printed and bound in the UK by BookPrintingUK
Website: www.bookprintinguk.com

FOREWORD

Welcome, Reader!

For Young Writers' latest competition, **Once Upon A Time**, we gave school children nationwide the tricky challenge of writing a story with a beginning, middle and an end in just 100 words, and they rose to the challenge magnificently!

We chose stories for publication based on style, expression, imagination and technical skill. The result is this entertaining collection full of diverse and imaginative mini sagas, which is also a delightful keepsake to look back on in years to come.

Here at Young Writers our aim is to encourage creativity in children and to inspire a love of the written word, so it's great to get such an amazing response, with some absolutely fantastic stories. This made it a tough challenge to pick the winners, so well done to Ryan Huntley who has been chosen as the best author in this anthology. You can see the winning story on the front cover.

I'd like to congratulate all the young authors in Once Upon A Time – Staffordshire & Worcestershire – I hope this inspires them to continue with their creative writing. And who knows, maybe we'll be seeing their names on the best seller lists in the future...

Jenni Bannister

Editorial Manager

CONTENTS

RIDGEWAY MIDDLE SCHOOL, REDDITCH

ST ANDREW'S CE PRIMARY SCHOOL, STAFFORD

ST DOMINIC'S PRIORY SCHOOL, STONE

ST ELIZABETH'S RC PRIMARY SCHOOL, TAMWORTH

ST JAMES CE PRIMARY SCHOOL, RUGELEY

YARLET SCHOOL, STAFFORD

THE MINI SAGAS

The Disaster

One hot summer's day, Lucy and Lara were playing in the paddling pool. But out of nowhere, Lara said, 'Shall we go on an adventure?'
Lucy said, 'Why and where?'
'To the jungle. Also we might meet your favourite animal.'
'Why, what's my favourite animal then?'
Lara said, 'A snake!
'I can't wait!'
Off they went to the jungle. Guess what the first animal they found was: a snake! Lucy shouted, 'Get a picture!' All of a sudden, they felt a rumble. They both fell over. It was a stampeding bear. They ran home quickly. At last they were home.

Ashli-Mai Hulse (10)
Churnet View Middle School, Leek

The Black Shadow

I left the warm hot sun and headed to the cold, damp rain. I hated anything cold or wet. I had to go to England. I had to stay with Dad who I'd not seen for six years. I wasn't sure I was going to like it. When I arrived I saw a black shadow and heard deep howls. That night, I heard the same howl, what was it? So I jumped down from my window and I saw a black, furry creature... Since that night that memory has haunted me. I hope that never happens to you!

Lois Heath (10)
Churnet View Middle School, Leek

Dragons, Quests And Monsters

One day in Green Bays, Warden Trump was telling his young boy Dominic off. But Dominic wasn't paying attention, because all he had on his mind was the brilliant scout challenge. This magnificent challenge was going all around Green Bays. Everyone was wanting to join, but poor Dominic was not allowed because his father didn't care about it until one day, Warden Trump had a use for the challenge. But then he was told to enter the challenge for one purpose, to capture the Incas – the Incas is a beast with powers. This was his mission.

Thomas Clough (10)
Churnet View Middle School, Leek

I'm Lost

'Dad can we go to the park and go on the swings and slide?' Dad said he was going to get us some dinner. However, there was a man with a black fabric jacket on... He took me away as I cried, 'Dad! Dad!' Then *bang*, the van door had been slammed shut. Time went by and when we got to the black hole in London I shouted, 'Anyone here? Is anyone here? Please help me, please.' Then I realised Mum worked next door. So, all I had to do was get out of the chains...

Kin Critchlow (10)
Churnet View Middle School, Leek

Stunts Go Wrong!

One day at 4am Jack woke up and looked at his clock and stormed out of bed. He realised he was meant to leave the house at 3am. He shouted, 'Mum, Dad, get out of bed lazy.' Once he had got out the house, they went to pick up Zack and his parents and the motorbikes. They travelled to the race track. Zack and Jack entered a stunt bike race for money and fame. Once they arrived, they went straight to the pit lane and raced. All of the race went perfectly.

Jack Turner (10)
Churnet View Middle School, Leek

The Lost Child

On the 20th of April 2003, Kevingen Peterson was all alone, in the station of the London Underground. He kept on asking people, he got no answers or luck. Then he sat down on a rusty bench, then a man started walking towards him and said, 'Hello, is your name Kevingen? I know where your mum is!'
Then Kevin shouted, 'Who are you?'
Then the man pointed to his mum. Kevingen ran up towards her and gave her a massive hug and a kiss. Then the man vanished. Was it real or was this all a dream? No one knows!

Jacob Goldstraw (10)
Churnet View Middle School, Leek

Medieval Times – Under Water In A Time Machine

In Medieval times, but under water in a time machine, there was a man called Charlie Clough and his friend was called Kin. 'You should be careful,' said Charlie. But Kin was already gone. 'Good job time machine.' The time machine had got everything he needed. He wanted to head back but he could not, he was stranded forever but he took a chance and swam as fast as he could down to the time machine. As he was nearly out of breath he got to the time machine and headed back home. It was night, he went to bed.

Macauley Earth (10)
Churnet View Middle School, Leek

The Runaway

One summer's morning, Ashli and Jessica came into my class to get me. All of my classmates said, 'Lara, where are you going?'
I said, 'I don't know.'
As Jess and Ashli took me out, I said, 'Where we going?'
They said at the same time, 'We're sneaking out of school to go on an adventure.'
I asked, 'How are we going to get past the people at the front office?'
'We'll go out one of the doors that lead outside. Mum's just around the corner, waiting for us,' said Ashli.
I shouted, 'Cool!' Soon we were walking in the jungle...

Lara-Mai Beaumont (10)
Churnet View Middle School, Leek

Tiger Attack!

Oh no, I was on an adventure and I was being attacked by a tiger! It just exploded out of a bush and began to pounce. I was so scared, but luckily I had a lasso. So I tied it to the tree and got closer to the tiger. My heart was pounding and just as the tiger opened its mouth, I wrapped the rope around its neck, trying not to hurt it. I loosened the rope but not all the way, and then I ran...

Jasmine Hutchinson (9)
Churnet View Middle School, Leek

Tropical Island Talk!

One glorious summer day on the beach of Miami, Autumn was sunbathing under the hot summer sun when all of a sudden... the waves got bigger and the sun got hotter until... *splash!* The waves collapsed over her sending her adrift in the North Atlantic Ocean! 'I've been here for hours, I really need a rest!'
Autumn glanced up ahead with the sky shimmering down on her and up ahead was a tropical island! Autumn swam and swam until she reached the island. Autumn walked over to a monkey but tripped and the monkey said, 'Hi!'

Jess Hurst
Churnet View Middle School, Leek

Ted!

Once upon a time there was a boy called Bob who lived in New York. He lived with his best friend who was a teddy called Ted. Ted worked at Tesco and Bob at Mulbery Leaves.
One warm summer's day Ted was walking to work when a man called Paul kidnapped Ted and kept him for his son. Ted was stuck and playing hide-and-seek when he saw a catflap! Ted ran for it and ran to see Bob. Ted told Bob. Bob was angry and beat up Paul. Bob and Ted lived in peace.

Joshua Nadin (9)
Churnet View Middle School, Leek

World War II

A beautiful coastline of the Normandy beaches where peace used to be known, until now! The Germans started war with France but after a few weeks England suddenly got involved and the war really began. The guns fired every second and then I caught up with Milan and Geoff. We saluted to freedom and then charged off the boat and into formations. Suddenly a German soldier, Barney the Beast, came out of a bush like a jackal. So I shoved Geoff and Milan into a bush and then reached for my gun but they caught and then strangled me.

Joe Knight (10)
Churnet View Middle School, Leek

A Boy Who Crashes A Tractor Into A Farm

A little boy called Tod hated everybody in his family. One morning his mum Laura and his dad Ted woke up and went downstairs. There was a big tractor in the living room so they shouted Bob (brother) and Kathrin (sister). They ran down the stairs and screamed, his dad Ted looked in the tractor and found Tod sitting in the seat. He pulled him out and phoned for an ambulance. He took him to hospital, he was in a coma for two days, and three days later he sadly died. His mum and family were sad forever.

Zack Weekes (10)
Churnet View Middle School, Leek

Under The Sea

Once upon a time there was a parade and a mermaid princess was there. Then a witch appeared and she caught the mermaid princess and trapped her in her gloomy castle. Next a prince found her and rescued her and then the witch came back, she saw them and they had a battle. The poor mermaid just watched and then the prince and mermaid princess got married. Before long the witch felt bad because of all she did to the princess mermaid and then she wanted to be good. Soon she decided to go to their wedding to show care.

Bethany Fletcher (6)
Colwich CE Primary School, Stafford

The Tiger Who Ate His Friends

Once upon a time there lived a tiger who was hungry and he saw his friends but he didn't recognise them so he tried to eat them. He chased them and then he hid behind some grass and jumped onto the deer. Then he ate it but he was still hungry. Next he ate the mouse. Luckily the mouse had children. The kids grew up so he had friends again. This time he didn't eat them. They played all day long because he behaved this time.

Abigail Urban (6)
Colwich CE Primary School, Stafford

The Tree Arguing

Once upon a time there were lots of fairies living in an enchanted forest, it was very old! One day the fairies went out flying. When they came down they could find lots of trees, but they couldn't find theirs anywhere. So they started to cry.
Soon they realised that they were in the wrong forest, so they flew up and away in to the right forest and found their home. The fairy godmother made more holes in the tree, so all of the fairies were super-duper happy and they weren't arguing anymore.

Olivia Marie Stamp (6)
Colwich CE Primary School, Stafford

My Life In The Army

I was sprinting through the forest when I saw the bull. My spear slipped, the boar charged and I got my scar. At last I was a man! I got home, someone told me I had to go to war.
I hacked, I cut and fought, I didn't give up. The Trojans bought a horse and attacked us. At last, we surrendered then we started on the long voyage home. So they found us and conquered our outskirts. Our city still held out against the Trojans that wanted us so badly. Although they knew they couldn't get us...

Kate Hurley (6)
Colwich CE Primary School, Stafford

The Seven Little Mermaids

Once upon a time there were seven little mermaid girls, they were sisters. One day Ariel was talking to the queen but they got stuck in the castle. Ariel got out but the queen didn't get out of the castle. A prince came along and saw the queen at the window. The prince broke in and saved the queen. The queen wanted to thank the prince but she was too scared to say thanks. So she asked Ariel to marry him. Ariel married the prince and they lived happily ever after.

Irene May Threlfall (6)
Colwich CE Primary School, Stafford

Untitled

Once, in a faraway land, there was a shiny new palace. It was yellow and there was a princess and her parents crashed in a ship and were missing. She wanted to find them. She thought they might be in the ocean in a dark cave so she swam to the cave and in that cave was a hidden chest with a crown on it. She thought, *this might be the cave that my parents lived in*. She heard a noise and it was her parents, her mother and father. They all lived in a new palace with servants.

Isabel Barnes (6)
Colwich CE Primary School, Stafford

The Secret

Once upon a time there lived a prince, a princess and king. One day the king had a spell and he was going to put it on the princess to make her a slave. The prince was on his way when the king locked the door! The prince had an idea. He went round the archer guarding the princess and discovered the door was locked. The princess said, 'No!' The king went to the lab. He made a spell to stop the prince. Too late, the prince broke down the door and killed the naughty king.

Samuel Taylor (6)
Colwich CE Primary School, Stafford

Little Red Riding Hood

Once upon a time there was a girl who was going to Grandma.
Then she went into the woods and she saw a fairy and killer wolf.
The girl made it to Grandma, the girl said, 'What big ears you have.'
The girl said, 'What big eyes you have.'
The last statement, 'What big teeth you have.'
'Argh, you aren't Grandma! It isn't Grandma, it's the wolf!' The
woodcutter threw the wolf into the forest, then Grandma and the girl
lived happily ever after.

Daniel Deakin (6)
Colwich CE Primary School, Stafford

Untitled

Once upon a time there were three little pigs who wanted to run
into the forest. In the forest there was a beautiful village and in the
village the three pigs found a transformer. The transformer picked
up a house and threw it, it set on fire. After that they started a fight
and the transformer shot one pig but it did not hurt. Meanwhile one
pig defeated him and all the people watched it. The first pig wanted
to celebrate because he'd defeated the transformer and up came a
trophy.

Max Farish (6)
Colwich CE Primary School, Stafford

The Mermaid And The Fish

Once upon a time there lived a mermaid. She was rich. She lived on water in a palace. One day she went out for a walk. When she came back she couldn't find her home. She cried and cried until she found a scary fish. 'I am scared,' she said and swam as fast as she could. She found her home, 'I am so happy,' she said. She invited her friends round for a party. She found the fish at the door. The fish was angry so the mermaid did not invite it in.

Lucy Rudman (6)
Colwich CE Primary School, Stafford

Untitled

The Superman got lost in the forest but the other man saved him. A bad guy put the men to sleep. He did this because he wanted to be mean. The men woke up and saw him. The Superman put the bad guy in jail just in time. The bad guy was sad, he was in jail.

Liam Lewis-Brown (5)
Colwich CE Primary School, Stafford

Busy Bees And Harriet

Once upon a time there lived a mermaid and a monster. The pretty mermaid went to a castle. It was glittery. Naughty Monster Max tried to steal pretty Elee's treasure. She found Monster Max was stealing, the solider fish came to see what was happening. They did not know and then the queen locked up Monster Max and they had a party and the treasure was taken back.

Harriet Ferguson (6)
Colwich CE Primary School, Stafford

The Mermaid And The Dog

Once upon a time there was a mermaid and a dog and the dog wanted to bite the mermaid. The dog went to the mermaid but the dog could not bite her. He went back and tried again. He still could not do it because the mermaid was too quick. The dog went back the next day but the dog couldn't bite her because she was super fast that time. The dog tried again and the mermaid was super speedy. He went back and he did it that time. She got hurt that time.

Rebecca Vaughan (6)
Colwich CE Primary School, Stafford

Princess Mermaid

Ariel is a princess mermaid, she saw a prince and her dad said not to marry him. She was sad, because her dad said, 'No!' So she swam away and found another prince. She swam to the prince and said, 'Can I marry you?' Then the prince and the princess kissed. Before long they married and lived happily ever after.

Jessica Farrant (6)
Colwich CE Primary School, Stafford

Body Swap!

Far away, a girl called Rino, the queen and a witch lived. Rino got to live in the palace for a week on the condition that she was a maid. The queen coughed on some days and sneezed on others. One day, Rino decided she wanted to be a pug. It would be lovely to exist in a different point of view! Once, the queen got sick, Rino felt really bad. Rino asked if she could do anything and the queen answered, she could be a pug and she would take her parts! There was some magic, Rino was a pug!

Ella-Mae Chilton-Piper (10)
Eton Park Junior School, Burton-On-Trent

Humans Vs Aliens – The World's Most Amazing Quiz

Once upon a time, there was a man called Dave, then aliens came to Earth and asked Dave for a quiz battle in the houses of Parliament. Then the alien called Borg stepped forward and said, 'If you beat me I will leave Earth but if I beat you we will take over Earth.'

After the fourth question Dave was losing 3-1. He was scared he might have to work for the aliens. Then Borg got the rest wrong, Dave got them all right. The final score was 10-3 so Dave won and Borg left Earth, sad about his loss.

Dylan Elden-Day (10)
Eton Park Junior School, Burton-On-Trent

The Haunted Mirror

One night, there was a babysitter and a child. The babysitter went to get her chips from the cellar when she saw a ghost through the window. She grabbed the chips and ran. Then she went to get ketchup and saw the ghost with a knife! The babysitter grabbed the ketchup and ran. The girl went to get mayonnaise but didn't come back for hours. She went to see if anything had happened. The girl was gone and the knife had blood on it! The parents came, and there were only mirrors. Which meant the ghost was behind them...

Faiza Kausar (10)
Eton Park Junior School, Burton-On-Trent

Jo's Sparkle

One day a family found a Christmas fairy kept in the loft of their new house. The family were thrilled to have her but the fairy wasn't. She was very upset, she had no more sparkle. She cried and cried. Suddenly there was a gentle tap on the door and in came a beautiful fairy flapping her stunning wings. 'Do you want your sparkle back?' whispered Amy.
'Yes!' cried Jo. Amy went over to Jo and sprinkled her with sparkle. Now she could bring happiness to the family by fluttering to the top of the tree where she belonged!

Sumayah Mahmood (9)
Eton Park Junior School, Burton-On-Trent

The Magic Carrot

Once upon a time in the future, a young robot lived in Wales on a delightful summer's day. Then the robot got out of his teleportation car to go fishing. So he got out his fishing rod and put it in the water. After 12 hours of waiting he caught something that wasn't a fish, he caught a carrot. This was no ordinary carrot, it was a magical carrot that kept sparkling. The robot ate the vegetable and started to dance rapidly.
After a few years he stopped and then he broke down. The robot fell to the floor, exhausted.

Ellisse Marie Bloomer (10)
Eton Park Junior School, Burton-On-Trent

Troublemaker

One day, on the 13th December, when it was snowing fast, a doctor called Dean went clothes shopping. Whilst Dean was looking at a T-shirt, someone slipped a different T-shirt into his bag when he wasn't looking. He wandered off, because he wasn't interested. Suddenly, the alarms blared and Dylan the manager of TK Maxx came to him and searched Dean. Surprised, he handed over the shirt and in payment, he had to work for the day in the shop. For free! From then on, Dean always kept an eye on his bag, to make sure it never happened again.

T-Jay Meredith (10)
Eton Park Junior School, Burton-On-Trent

Untitled

Once there was a boy named Dan. One day he got dared to go to Hauntvilla, a haunted house. Dan forgot to take his cross as protection and ran into a monster! It chased him. Dan saw Scooby-Doo and his friends. Fred decided to stop the monster from causing harm. Dan's job was to pull the lever. When Fred uncovered the monster, the gang said, 'Mr Lapiz!'
'I was trying to scare people away and I would have gotten away with it too if it wasn't for you meddling kids.' Dan went back to school and told the story.

Aman Adil (10)
Eton Park Junior School, Burton-On-Trent

The Mermaid And The Crystal

Once upon a time, under the blue sea, there was a mermaid. She protected a magical crystal that gave light and power under the sea. One day Daisy found that the crystal had been stolen! But then around the small pillar she saw some tracks in the sand, shaped like suckers! So Daisy told herself to find the crystal. What if it was the mean octopus? Daisy followed the mysterious tracks to a cave with light there. She went in and saw the mean octopus. Then she sneaked in to get the crystal, to give power back again.

Brodie Jayne Stretton (10)
Eton Park Junior School, Burton-On-Trent

Earthquake Escape

There was once a day when Emma, an orphan, lived in an orphanage. The mischievous little girl almost got kicked out. One day she started running around the coloured building being chased by a teacher. Suddenly the floor started to rumble and the drill began to start. An earthquake! The teacher ran away alone. Emma ran onto the street. As she ran out on the path a building collapsed. There wasn't a way through the rubble. Obviously there had to be a solution. Not far away there was a path leading to safety. Emma sprinted quickly just before another building fell.

Sofia Shaheen (10)
Eton Park Junior School, Burton-On-Trent

Haunted House

'I dare you to go into 13 Mahogany Street tonight.' As I walked into the crooked house, I heard footsteps coming towards me. They were getting louder, continuously until they disappeared. *Slam!* The door locked behind me. Fear filled my heart. I tried pulling the door repeatedly but it was no use. In relief, I found a chair and smashed it against the door. I got out and fog surrounded my feet and I saw it mould figures. One looked like my cousin that died two years ago. I ran into my house, I was never going there again.

Tanisha Gilbert-Gallagher (10)
Eton Park Junior School, Burton-On-Trent

Race To Witch Mountain

A new glistening potion had been discovered, which made you strong and healthy. Both evil Drake and good Josh were racing to Witch Mountain. When he got there, Drake tried to shoot Josh but Josh dodged the bullets. A fight started during which Drake fell off the mountain to his death. Josh was happy that he survived the fight. He got the glorious potion and made his way home off Witch Mountain with a broken arm and a very bruised leg. Josh gave half to the poorly people and kept half for himself.

Yasser Shahzad (10)
Eton Park Junior School, Burton-On-Trent

Superman To The Rescue

Once there were robberies every day. There was a person called Superman. Superman was a very clever person who discovered that the robber was going to do something really intelligent. The robber was going to steal from the most expensive jewellery shop. The burglar entered the shop, very cunningly. At night, when it was pitch-black, Superman was hiding so he could catch the robber. As quick as a flash, he entered and pressed the alarm button. He jumped on him, the police arrived and he was jailed forever. Superman was the hero and he also got a reward.

Saif Ali (10)
Eton Park Junior School, Burton-On-Trent

The Ghost Of Haunted Park!

One day a girl called Sophie discovered she was going to the best theme park ever, called Haunted Park. She was really excited. 'Thanks parents!' she exclaimed. Sophie saw the blood-curdling Ghost Ride and immediately wanted to go on it. However, when she got off an invisible ghost followed her. Sophie told her family but they didn't believe her, she decided to solve it herself. *What should I do?* thought Sophie, *no one believes me.* However, all she needed to do was go back on the Ghost Ride again and trap the ghost again.

Libby-Jo Neal (10)
Eton Park Junior School, Burton-On-Trent

The Curse

Once upon a time there was a princess who lived in a castle. She was cursed but didn't know what the curse was. She grew up to be a beautiful and flawless girl. One day she met a prince and was mesmerised. She gazed out the window staring at him. Luckily, the next day the prince requested to marry her, however she was aware of the curse. She took the risk and agreed to go. She stepped out the castle and turned pale. She fell on the floor, went to sleep and never woke up again.

Mohammed Muhaimeen Nafees (10)
Eton Park Junior School, Burton-On-Trent

The Dinosaur Ate My Homework

One glorious day, in a town called Springfield, a boy (Ben) forgot his homework. Ben's teacher was angry and asked Ben where his homework was. Ben replied, 'A dinosaur ate it!'
The teacher mumbled, 'Show proof.'
The next day Ben came with a T-rex, big as a monster truck. Ben thought of the T-rex tearing Miss Naughton's head off. The T-rex had muscles like no other, stone-like back and spikes sharper than a samurai sword. Out of nowhere, the dinosaur broke its head through the roof and ate Miss Naughton. From then on people never said Ben lied.

Milad Niassa (10)
Eton Park Junior School, Burton-On-Trent

The Cursed Bubblegum

A young lady named Lily snapped her necklace because it wasn't fitting her neck. She went to the jewellery shop, 'The Ruby's' which was famous around the city.
She met a considerate friend who offered her some bubblegum. However, the bubblegum was cursed! When she went home, she looked in the mirror and it sucked Lily in for thirty years. When it had passed, she came out and paid a visit to the jewellery shop. When she asked kindly, the jewellery maker explained he would deliver it in four days. Lily was outraged that her necklace was still not fixed!

Imaan Iqbal (10)
Eton Park Junior School, Burton-On-Trent

Hauntville Hotel

In the night the Hauntville Hotel changes. Everything becomes eerie and frightening...
Long ago, a tourist called Ariel was sent to Hauntville to explore it. Ariel had to spend some creepy nights in the hotel, however she didn't know what surprises were waiting for her. It was black and dingy now. Ariel was sleepy so she went to bed early. Ariel slept for so long that she didn't know that the ghosts and spirits were planning to kill her. When the clock struck midnight Ariel disappeared and never came back. Hauntville was shut down forever...

Simran Abid (10)
Eton Park Junior School, Burton-On-Trent

The Tooth Fairy Meets...

The 8th of June there was a girl, her name was Sophie and her tooth fell out that night and she was so happy that the tooth fairy was coming...

That night the little fairy flew to Sophie's home but when the fairy flew inside Sophie's home, Sophie woke up and saw Jess the fairy. Jess the fairy said hello and Sophie asked, 'You are a fairy aren't you?'

'Yes,' said Jess, 'follow me.'

So Jess took Sophie to Jess' home and she met Jack, Tom and Ben and they were playing.

Tia Weston (9)
Newstead Primary Academy, Stoke-On-Trent

The Evil Kebab

Once upon a time there lived a little boy called Rai. He went to a restaurant and ordered a chicken kebab. Then he started going green. He looked like a lizard. He started to crash the restaurant down and all the people were running around. Then Spider-Man came to town. The town screamed, 'Hooray, it's Spider-Man.' Spider-Man shouted, 'I know his weakness, it's hip hop. I need to phone some hip hop singers.' The town singers came and started singing. Suddenly the lizard started to dance, the lizard was finally sent to hip hop dancing and got 1,000 dollars.

Joshua Barnett & Henri Oliver Lowe (10)
Newstead Primary Academy, Stoke-On-Trent

The Birthday Surprise

One day in a small isolated village, there was a young princess called Aurora. She lived with her dad. Her mum had died from illness when Aurora was only two years old. This left her devastated. On the morning of her seventh birthday she woke up by the sound of footsteps, she went downstairs to find a parcel. The parcel, which was addressed to her, was a unicorn, the best present ever! Aurora called her unicorn Bob. Bob loved Aurora, Aurora loved Bob. He had a pink moustache and a purple sparkly horn. A few hours later he wasn't there...

Lilie Mae Cheadle (10)
Newstead Primary Academy, Stoke-On-Trent

Harry Potter And The Philosopher's Stone

'That Dumbledore is a fool!' drawled Lucius Malfoy, turning to Draco.
'I agree Father, bringing in all of those filthy Mudbloods!' said Draco. He agreed that Dumbledore was a fool and an idiot but bringing Mudbloods in was too much. He hated Harry more than Dumbledore though because he was so famous and was always getting looks from others. Snape was amazing and was the best teacher at Hogwarts to Malfoy but he was devoted to Dumbledore, as well as Professor McGonagall, one of the worst teachers at school. And that lumbering oaf Hagrid, how they would suffer before him!

Lily Peasegood (10)
Newstead Primary Academy, Stoke-On-Trent

Tracey In Trouble!

Tracey sat on the park bench, lazily throwing stones into the pond. Mum had warned her to never ever go into the field because kidnappers and nasty men were there. She decided that nobody would find out... She quietly skipped to the field and collapsed on the sweet, fresh grass. Suddenly, there was a yell. An ugly man clutching a beer can ran over to her, his arms held out. Tracey ran. She sprinted up the road and into her mum's arms. Tears poured down her face. 'I will never disobey you again, Mum,' she said and Mum laughed.

Chloe May Tolley (10)
Newstead Primary Academy, Stoke-On-Trent

Mr Bunny And Earth

Once upon a time in a faraway land with strange creatures, like half-bunnies and half-fairies, lived a little bunny who was sent to a different planet named Earth. 'Where am I?' Suddenly a group of strange animals appeared.
'Who are you? What do you want?'
'Sorry, where are our manners, I'm Miss Kitty and this is Little Pup. Sorry we scared you but we have never seen a creature like you before.'
'I'm Mr Bunny, the bunny fairy. Do you want to be friends?'
'Oh yes please, after all I'm now a creature like you!'

Abigail Paige Ellis (10)
Newstead Primary Academy, Stoke-On-Trent

My Horror Story

I awoke by the sound of sudden lightning. I looked at my alarm clock and noticed that it was only 4.30am. I tried to nod back off but it wasn't worth it. Then I heard footsteps creeping towards my door, so I bravely got out of bed and opened the door. Ahead of me stood a shadowy figure in the distance. I stood there trembling with fear. I suddenly felt the urge to grab my flashlight. I took a deep breath in and shone the torch ahead of me. I turned around, my eyes still closed, then I opened them...

Madison Paige Taylor (10)
Newstead Primary Academy, Stoke-On-Trent

Untitled

Dear Diary, today was terrible. I found out my best friend really isn't! She's been lying since her face appeared on the Earth, which is twelve years and four months (to be precise). So she told me she lived in a castle, nope – no wonder she bit my head off when I asked to go to her house! She said she had over a million pounds! She doesn't even have a bank account! Megan lies about so many more things. I hate friends so I will see you tomorrow, love from the amazing Miss Bella Clair Ross – the best!

Rebecca Cooper (10)
Parkside Middle School, Bromsgrove

The City Of The Dead!

Josh came back from school and had just got bullied. Suddenly he saw and heard the ground was shaking. He sprinted as fast as lightning back home. But... his whole house was full of aliens and zombies. He was startled and ran into the deep, dark, gloomy woods. He grabbed a shotgun BBgun. *Bang!* He shot a zombie dead in its heart, his hair was raising and his spine was tingling. He knew one was coming! He camped in a military base. He saw a zombie come in and it stabbed him. He lay there dead...

Yousuf Beegun (10)
Parkside Middle School, Bromsgrove

There's A Clown In My Room

Once upon a time, there was a girl. Luckily, she was moving house to a mansion full of mysteries. When they arrived a shudder went down her spine! She went to take a few classy pictures of her new bedroom. She took one of the door, then of the room. Shockingly, a scary clown stood there, but only in the photo, so she snapped another one. The clown was closer and again its face was there. Then he explained; he had to act frightening as he was just a friendly clown.

Isabel Kate O'Neill (10)
Parkside Middle School, Bromsgrove

Once Upon A Change

Alex decided to visit the lake. As he crossed over the bridge he fell into the water. Clinging onto the beams, a frightening voice boomed out, 'Who is under my bridge?' Alex did not dare answer. As he peeped out, he saw an enormous troll making a portal. He finished and ugly trolls scrambled out of the hole destroying everything in their path. To Alex's surprise three billy goats clumsily rushed over the bridge. Alex bravely chased away the trolls, closed up the portal then climbed out of the lake. He had changed the story.

Holly Lindsay (10)
Parkside Middle School, Bromsgrove

Poseidon's Revenge

In the city of Rome, a shark, Hydra, was swimming in the ocean. It was made from the mighty Poseidon. All Romans that tried had perished miserably, they thought it was impossible. But there was one Roman who could do it, the hero of Rome, Julius Caesar, the emperor's son. He had to cross the Red Sea to find the killer deep. He found it with Poseidon. He gripped his sword and got ready for a fight. He sliced and chopped but the heads grew back and he learned from Hercules to use a torch and he was victorious.

Benjamin David Arnold (10)
Parkside Middle School, Bromsgrove

Sticky Ninja Invades Raccoon Land

One day Roxie and Ronnie were playing at the park, then there was a tornado and there stood a Ninja. They ran home to tell their mother but the sticky Ninja followed them home. Roxie and Ronnie told the Raccoon CIA. Then the Ninja smelt some of Mother Raccoon's porridge and ran to the house to have some. The Raccoon CIA fought him but he escaped and took Ronnie but... Roxie wouldn't stand for that so Roxie punched, kicked, smacked and headbutted the Ninja until he was dead. The Raccoon CIA took the Ninja away, never to be seen again.

Rachel Bradley (9)
Parkside Middle School, Bromsgrove

The End!

It was a Saturday night and Joe was watching TV, when all of a sudden a news flash popped up. 'All men between the age of 11 and 31 must go to the nearest launch pad.' Joe quickly gathered all his prized possessions and made it to the Californian launch pad. He got on the rocket and made it to the moon Europa. The mission was to see whether people could survive on the planet. They searched and searched but nothing. All of a sudden a huge wave came crashing down and everyone got washed up on the shore...

Maddie Clews (10)
Parkside Middle School, Bromsgrove

The Big Bad...!

It was a Wednesday and Olivia was walking over the roof when she saw a crack on the roof. So she tried to jump over the crack instead, she fell into the prison! All of a sudden the monkeys' eyes went red, they chased Olivia into a jail where an evil monkey lay on a concrete bed. It sat up and shouted, 'There's a strange person in here, help!'
'Calm down, I'm not bad person, I'm just a young girl and I have fallen into this horrible jail. I really want to go home!'
What happened next?...

Emily Christine Schofield (10)
Parkside Middle School, Bromsgrove

The Old Man

Once upon a time there was an old man who was going to die. His children were very upset because he had cancer. One of the sons had an idea, he said, 'Let's take Dad to an imaginary land.'
'Good idea.'
'Dad, want to go somewhere?'
'Alright,' said Dad.
So the oldest child drove them through a portal and found themselves in a land where the ground was made of sweets. The sky was made of crisps and the buildings were made of chocolate. They had a great time.

Jack McNaughton (10)
Parkside Middle School, Bromsgrove

Sweet 16

At the end of the summer year Meg was throwing a sweet 16 party and inviting all her friends. Meg, Kiera and Becca were going shopping for dresses. Kiera bought a purple strapless dress, Becca bought a one shoulder magenta dress and Meg bought a strapless pink ball gown. After the girls got their dresses they went to get some cupcakes for the party. They all went back to Meg's to get ready. All the guests started to arrive and everyone was looking and commenting on Meg's dress. After the party Kiera and Becca stopped over at Meg's house.

Rebecca Moncrieff (10)
Parkside Middle School, Bromsgrove

The Girl With A Pet Dragon

Time to get some eggs for my mother, oops, I must have dropped one. Finally home, time to give these eggs to my mum.
Two days later. What! A baby dragon! I better hide you from my mum. You can hide in my garage, for now. I think I'll call you Ocean, the water dragon. Almost done and finished, your very own home. I love you so much Ocean. Time to ride you, Ocean, now don't be scared, it's all right. Yay, I've got a pet dragon called Ocean, Ocean the water dragon. Who I love so much!

Amy Alice Folger (10)
Parkside Middle School, Bromsgrove

The Dancing Horse

Once upon a time there was a horse named Walter. One day he was minding his own business eating hay and then his farmer (Callum) came along. He checked on Walter and said, 'Good day, good day.' Suddenly Walter saw a bottle with some blue bubbling, he decided to open the bottle. He drank it all. While Farmer Callum was refilling the hay, Walter swallowed all the liquid and with one bang he was dancing with Farmer Callum to Tango. He put a rose in his mouth and soon they were married.

Ellie Louise Hayward (10)
Parkside Middle School, Bromsgrove

The Dying Brothers And The Fairy

Once upon a time there were two brothers in a hot, lonely desert and they needed some more food and water. Suddenly a fairy came down from the sky and supplied them with food and water for days and it said, 'I will come back when you run out because I don't want you to die.' Then they held a banquet and they lived until they got old. Then the fairy chose the next pair and the process kept on repeating and the fairy and the pair of brothers today lived happily ever after in the hot, lonely, quiet desert.

Lukas Mykyta Green (10)
Parkside Middle School, Bromsgrove

The End Of The World!

One night Tom and his family were watching the news. But what was said was not good! 'The world is going to end,' said Tom's mom. 'You must get up at six o'clock.'
'OK,' said Tom, almost falling asleep.
Tom's mum set the alarm, car horn, band and turned the TV up on full volume. Because Tom was always an hour late he woke up at seven o'clock! His parents were packing everything up. Then Tom's parents went downstairs for breakfast. Tom came downstairs for breakfast but his parents had left him alone...

Lucy Kent (9)
Parkside Middle School, Bromsgrove

The Great Adventure

There lived a boy called Zac. Zac absolutely loved playing with electronics! One day, when Zac was playing around with the TV wires, he started to feel a bit dizzy. When suddenly, he passed out! After a while, he woke up and found himself on Mars. There was nothing there, he had nothing except his lucky teddy. Just then, he dropped his lucky teddy. The only thing he had with him. This was his absolute favourite teddy! He took it everywhere. What will Zac do to save his precious teddy?

Grace Perry (10)
Parkside Middle School, Bromsgrove

Greg And The Dark Forest

Greg was walking his dog (named Sam). He reached a weird forest that he'd never seen. They both decided to walk in to this mysterious forest. 'I've never been here before,' quietly mumbled Greg.
'Argh!' shouted Greg. 'We fell down a ditch.'
'Grrr,' grumbled Sam.
'Maybe I will tie your leash around the plant,' said Greg brightly. Greg looped the leash around the colossal plant as big as a bookshelf. 'Hooray!' shouted Greg. 'We are out of here.'
'Right, let's forget about the forest and let's go back home.'

Maxwell Mitchell (10)
Parkside Middle School, Bromsgrove

The Church!

One day two friends went to play out but noticed an unfamiliar path, so they decided to follow it. Suddenly, it stopped at a spooky looking church. 'Shall we go in?'
'OK.'
When they opened the door it slammed shut, so they tried to open it but they couldn't. They turned to go upstairs but they saw a ghost! They screamed and zoomed upstairs. Then they found another ghost, but this time froze with fear. 'Don't worry, I'm a friendly ghost. I will get you out of here!' And so he did. They thanked the ghost and went home...

Eden May Harrison (10)
Parkside Middle School, Bromsgrove

The One Hour War

Long ago there was a great explorer by the name of Johny-Jo. One cold December day he trekked up to Antarctica and claimed it as the UK's land. All around the world other countries were having huge debates on what just happened, they were so big it eventually turned into a war. All the countries were fighting non-stop for fifty-six minutes when a man, who nobody recognised, walked onto the battlefield and spoke aloud. 'Why did this start and when will it end?' When these words were spoken everyone stopped the war and it was over... or was it?

Caitlin E Kelly (10)
Parkside Middle School, Bromsgrove

The Two Aston Villa Fans

Once, there was a boy who loved playing football and his name was Callum. When he was at school nobody let him play with them but he was a good striker. He went home and started practising. Even all of his shots were on target.
The next day he asked them if he could play with them. After he asked about five times they said yes and he started playing. He scored ten in two minutes and they were shocked. Then they said, 'You can play every day.' They played day and night and they both supported Aston Villa.

Callum McDonald (11)
Parkside Middle School, Bromsgrove

35

I Was Playing Xbox

Once upon a time I was playing Xbox,when suddenly I got pulled into the TV. I dropped and flattened the FIFA 15 referee, Mickel Oliver. He stopped and said that I could play, so I put on an Aston Villa shirt and went on. Suddenly the floor opened and I dropped into a tube and fell into a limo with the prime minister. He chucked me onto the FIFA Street arena and I played with Messi, and I was number 21. Suddenly I got pulled back home and I went to bed.

Warric Michael Hastilow (9)
Parkside Middle School, Bromsgrove

Let's Go Places

One day, after school, a girl called Amy and a boy called George came out of high school and saw a box that had writing on the side that said, 'Let's Go Places'. They got in and pressed a button and ended up in... Egypt. They realised it was a time travel box! They pushed another button and *whoosh*, they were in America. They decided to go home so they pressed the red button and ended up in front of their house. They told their mum they'd gone to an after school club.

Keisha Ann Holdom (10)
Parkside Middle School, Bromsgrove

Best Friends

Once upon a time there were two girls, their names were Niamh and Mia, they went to the same school, that school was Park Side Middle School. They moved up into year six for the first time, they were very frightened. At school they got put into the same class. Mia had nobody to play with so she said to Niamh, 'Can I play with you?'

Niamh said, 'Yes.' Suddenly Niamh and Mia made a very, very strong bond together, they played and played until the end of the day. Then, they walked home together and played.

Niamh Banner (9)
Parkside Middle School, Bromsgrove

Who Knows...

Once, in the gutter, there lived a girl, Florence. A very joyful girl, who became a professional gymnast, swinging from branch to branch. But a mysterious phantom was looming across the land, unknown, stealing jewels and murdering the public. Florence had once had a father but she ran away after he smacked her. Now she had a creeping suspicion that he was targeting her. One day, when she was going to rehearsal, she saw a small glimpse of a night sky cloak peeping out from the old oak tree. Who was it? What was it? Young Florence might never know...

Amelia Duke (10)
Parkside Middle School, Bromsgrove

The Sound From Under My Bed...

One cold night, there was a loud rumble from the wardrobe. Tim, a young boy, was curled up in a ball petrified. Suddenly, there was heavy breathing coming from the wardrobe. Tim picked up the courage to go look. When he got to the dark wardrobe there was a loud creak! Amazed, Tim opened the wardrobe and saw nothing. He went back to bed with a horrifying look on his face. As he curled back up, he heard breathing once again, but this time from under his bed...

Tom Mahoney (10)
Parkside Middle School, Bromsgrove

The Pink Penguin

I'm different, I'm a pink penguin. They all make fun of me! Momma Penguin says I'm special. I was paddling in the sea to take my mind off it, when I felt something odd touch my flipper... I reached into the murky water, it was a baby pink egg! I nested on it for a few days, finally it hatched! It was... a baby pink penguin just like me! As it grew up, it became my best friend and we ignored the bullies. Different is beautiful!

Sophie Jane Turnbull (10)
Parkside Middle School, Bromsgrove

The Boy With Three Legs

I went to school one morning. Tripping over a stick, I grazed my leg. It really hurt. I went inside and the first aiders put an oily wipe on my leg. I was in a room by myself, when slowly, another leg sprouted up! I ambled about and tripped over. I didn't hurt myself this time because my new leg saved me! Everyone laughed at me and I fled home. I stayed at my house and had my education there until twenty years were over. Then, I went on an adventure to find my own kind. (I am still looking).

Daania Ahmad (10)
Parkside Middle School, Bromsgrove

The Time Snow White Married The Hulk

One unfortunate day some evil trolls took over Snow White's palace. But luckily Hulk heard her cry for help. Then he went to save her, he Hulk-smashed all the trolls far, far away. At that moment in time Snow White thought, *Hulk is so brave fighting those trolls I will ask him to go on a date.* To her astonishment he accepted. After they had a brilliant time on their date, they married, so if Snow White ever got into trouble again, Hulk would save her and they lived an almost safe life.

Matthew Thompson (10)
Parkside Middle School, Bromsgrove

Zombie Apocalypse

One day me, Dylan and Harvey were working at our work testing DNA on our subjects when Dylan said, 'I think we did something wrong.' All of a sudden *smash*, the glass broke.
'Where did he go?' Harvey said.
'We need to sort this out, we need to get a septic eye and spider's blood and we can cure this.'
'I think we have a septic eye somewhere.'
'OK, go and get the septic eye but we need spider blood.'
Two hours later they mixed it and... *bam!* They'd cured the apocalypse.

Cai Jackson (10)
Parkside Middle School, Bromsgrove

The Well

Once there were there people called Harvey, Alex and John. One sunny day they were meeting up at Harvey's house. When Alex reached Harvey's house Alex found that the door was wide open and thought to himself, *why would Harvey leave the door wide open?* Alex walked in and shouted, 'Harvey!' Harvey came walking down the stairs.
'Where's John?'
'He's there.'
They walked out of the door and walked outside. The ground started shaking. They dropped down this hole and found out that they were not alone. They looked around and saw a hooded figure. It stepped closer...

Kyle Read (10)
Parkside Middle School, Bromsgrove

Crunch

Russell crouched behind the old oak tree in sheer terror. In the orchard he knew he wasn't alone. In the distance he heard someone scream! The darker the sky got, death got closer. Russell listened. The scream... got louder. He listened. And listened. Then, he heard crunching on the leaves getting closer and closer. He started to get up, then he stopped dead. There was a black figure holding something... an axe? Whatever it was, he knew he had to keep dead still, and dead silent, otherwise he would be killed. The figure moved... *crunch... crunch... crunch... crunch... crunch...*

Scarlett Land (10)
Parkside Middle School, Bromsgrove

Teddies 'r' Us

Five special teddies were made and given to five boys that were twelve years old. They received the box in the post. There was a robbery and the boys were hostages but the teddies took care of that.
A few years later they became the elite team: 'Teddies 'r' Us'.
Later they got weapons such as swords, big goblets and electro beam shooters. The boys named them Bannas = monkey = leader, Fluff = gorilla, Bullet = raccoon, Snow = polar bear and Squawk = eagle. They became the biggest, most famous elite team in the world and they got some human recruits for back up.

Oakley Everton-Carr (10)
Parkside Middle School, Bromsgrove

The Hero Who Lost His Powers

There was once a hero with many talents. One day there was a bad guy who was horrible. The hero bumped into the bad guy and the bad guy had a thought. The bad guy made a deal with the hero that if he gave up his powers he wouldn't destroy the world. The hero thought and soon he said yes but the world got destroyed and he got his powers back... When he got his powers back he cured the world.

Tom Round (10)
Parkside Middle School, Bromsgrove

The Mouse That Didn't Like Cheese!

Once there was an unusual mouse because he didn't like cheese! He was called Sam. 'How could you not like cheese?' they said. 'You're hardly even a mouse!'
Sam would stay quiet but wish they'd all go away! One day Sam was walking alone across a meadow when suddenly he bumped into a lady mouse. The day went by and they became best friends. Kira told Sam she didn't like cheese! Sam told Kira he didn't like cheese either.
Nine years later... Sam and Kira were married and had seven children of their own who all didn't like cheese!

Natalie Bromhall (10)
Parkside Middle School, Bromsgrove

The Coconut Rescue!

Swoosh! went the wind as the sea got heavy! The island that my nan and grandad had been on for nearly 30 days was melting from the hot heat and they hadn't had anything to eat! I was getting worried. Suddenly, I got a text from my nan and it said, 'A coconut has started to talk to us.' Then I thought to myself, *what?* After that, I texted her back and said, 'Great!' I heard a big bang! The coconut fell and my nan and grandad lifted it up and chopped it in half and ate it together!

Hannah Louise Delaney (9)
Parkside Middle School, Bromsgrove

Bomb, Bomb!

'Ahh, take cover, bomb, bomb!' screamed Louise, hoping Mum would come, but where was she? 'Please Mother, please come,' but she didn't. 'I hope, I really, really hope the butcher's hasn't been b-b-b-bombed, it can't have been...'
The next few hours all Louise was able to do was sob, mumble and meander. After a little while longer, patiently waiting in the Shorter family's bomb shelter, the siren went off signalising Louise and Robert could nervously stroll out... 'The butcher's, it's gone!' Robert exclaimed. 'But look, there's Mother on the ground, and she's alive!' 'Mother, we both love you...' they cried!

Isobel Lindsay (10)
Parkside Middle School, Bromsgrove

Herbivore School

There once lived a T-rex whose name was Timmy. He was vegetarian so he couldn't attend Carnivore Academy (like the rest of the T-rexes). He signed up for Herbivore School! When Timmy arrived, all of the other dinosaurs were scared of him because he was a T-rex! This made Timmy very gloomy but he didn't show it. There was only one dinosaur that was not petrified of Timmy, her name was Tilly the triceratops. The head teacher Mr Bronco Brachiosaurus announced that Timmy was a vegetarian. Twenty years later Timmy proposed to Tilly and to his great surprise... 'Yes!'

Thomas Hasty (10)
Parkside Middle School, Bromsgrove

Bookworm

I had a worm that lived in my book. It said to me every day, 'I will be your bookmark.' The problem was he kept getting squashed! What was I going to do? I decided to make something so he could be comfy. But what? Then it hit me: I could make a jumper for him to wear. So I knitted a little red jumper with the letter 'W' on it. Now he is happy, he has a family too. Luckily, I have made them jumpers as well.

Mia Ashlee Hunt (10)
Parkside Middle School, Bromsgrove

The Cloud That Can't Fly

Once, on a Saturday morning, a man called James was walking down the street. He saw a cloud stuck on a tree. It was blowing tears all down its face! The man climbed up the tree and tried to shove him off the tree but he fell to the ground. The cloud desperately tried to fly but couldn't. James felt sorry for him. He tried to help with a trampoline, but the cloud came straight back down. The cloud was finally able to fly due to the man's help. He had now got rockets and wings to help him fly.

Luke Ringham (10)
Parkside Middle School, Bromsgrove

Ice Of The Unknown

One winter's day, Cait was ice skating on the local pond. Cait heard a noise and thought nothing of it. Suddenly, the noise became louder and louder. She was becoming worried. A crack appeared in the ice. She became more worried but she also became curious. Cait leaned in towards the crack to have a closer look. It seemed like the more Cait leaned in, the bigger the crack became. It was quite strange. As she leaned in closer, the more unbalanced she felt. When she got as close as she could to the crack a croaky voice said, 'Come.'

Paige Lucy Whitehouse (10)
Parkside Middle School, Bromsgrove

The Friendly Zombie

One misty night the Round family were gathered around a flaming dancing fire. Out of the ground came a thumping sound, and then the little zombie said... 'Hi, my name is Fred, and I'm a friendly zombie that rose from the dead!' He was really small, he was one metre tall. 'Wait there!' said Fred, 'I'm really friendly, just don't run because I'm very fun! I'm real,' he said, 'but I'm not tall, I'm not nasty, I'm really cool.' So they kicked him into the hole with a *bim bam boom!* And he jumped out with a bowl and spoon!

Ethan Kai Burke (10)
Parkside Middle School, Bromsgrove

Robo Invasion!

Six years ago in New York, New York, a lazy but extremely clever man called Christopher Grey made five robots to help him, so he went to his lab. One day he attempted to make them even more intelligent by changing their wire, but instead they went horribly evil. Then Christopher stupidly decided to check on them and they used their laser eyes to shoot him. Immediately he died, he was only the first victim. After they got into town the humans bombed them after watching the news, and that created a robot invasion...

Alfie Tait (10)
Parkside Middle School, Bromsgrove

Ellie's Best Party Ever

Once upon a time there was a girl called Ellie, her mum was called Amelia. Ellie's mum Amelia was planning a big party. Ellie's mum invited all of her friends. Ellie asked her mum if she was having a party, her mum replied, 'Maybe you might have a party.'
Ellie said, 'If I do have a party can I invite all of my friends?'
Amelia said, 'Yes you can.'
'Yippee!' said Ellie.
At her party Ellie said, 'This is the best party ever!' And all of her friends said the same.

Tristan Jack Gary Clifford (10)
Parkside Middle School, Bromsgrove

Untitled

All Randal could hear was laughter, laughter from the biggest bullies in school. Randal was the only book in Booklake Academy who had no words. 'I'll get you one day!' Randal shouted, well in his head; he couldn't talk.
The next day Randal ran across a book called Cameron. 'Hey, do you want to come and play?' he said. *No one ever talks to me*, Randal thought, so he just stood there smiling with his thumbs up. He felt words fill his pages. Suddenly he bumped into a bully, and shouted, 'Go away!' Then, he smiled and walked away.

Isabella Roberson (10)
Parkside Middle School, Bromsgrove

Terminator Genisys 17

'I wonder how Mom died?' said Jimmy.
'I miss her too,' replied Joey.
They travelled back in time to see if Mom could be saved. 'Help!' Jimmy cried, being sucked into the past.
They arrived in 1960, the year their mom died. As they were walking past, they spotted something nailed to a wall. It stated: *Wanted – reward $1000.* Then Jimmy screamed, 'That's Mom!'
'Kill her!' shouted a man.
They ran for their lives. Back to the time machine. They broke the time machine. It stated 2027. Then Jimmy saw blackness. He thought for a minute, 'I'm buried alive!'

Jaidan Shewell (10)
Parkside Middle School, Bromsgrove

Gangsta Granny's Grandson

One year ago Gangsta Granny stole the Crown Jewels, but not long after she passed away. Her grandson (Ben) took over the gangster role. Now Ben was trying to steal the biggest diamond in the world. The diamond was in a high security bunker. Ben dropped through the roof, he sprayed some hairspray into the air and discovered the lasers. He dodged the lasers, grabbed the diamond and *rrrrring!* 'Oh no!'...

Harry Parslow (10)
Parkside Middle School, Bromsgrove

The Giant Biscuit

One morning Leo spilt milk in his bakery on an ordinary biscuit, then he went home.
Next day, late afternoon, he came back and the biscuit was bigger, but then a customer came, he wanted a cake. The oven went *boom, crackle, fizz*. After, he served the customer. He went back to the biscuit and it was bigger but he hadn't touched the smoothed white milk. By the time the customer had gone it was dark and gloomy outside and the giant biscuit called Leo ran away scared and was on the run for two weeks!

Jordon Hodson-Walker (10)
Parkside Middle School, Bromsgrove

Snow White And The Seven Dwarfs

Once upon a time there lived a young girl named Snow White. She was called this because her skin was as white as snow. One day she decided to go for a walk but little did she know it would be gross and terrifying. After she had left, the evil queen ordered her huntsman to follow and kill Snow White. By the time the huntsman got there Snow White was picking some flowers. He couldn't kill her so he stabbed her instead. Snow White ran off screaming until she found a house of lovely dwarfs. Well, she thought they were lovely...

Natalie Wiggett (9)
Ridgeway Middle School, Redditch

Snow White And The Seven Dwarfs

Once upon a time there was a family. Unfortunately the mother died. The father remarried to a queen of another land. Snow White's new stepmother despised her. She hated her so much that she hatched a plan to kill her. Snow White had heard about her plan and went to find the dwarfs. Little did she know that they had been kidnapped! Eventually, she found identical people. They went over but they were not them, they were goblins employed by her stepmother. Later on they walked through the woods. One of them offered her a poisonous apple. She ate it...

Caitlin Grace Patricia Nesbitt (11)
Ridgeway Middle School, Redditch

The Grand Ball

One day three sisters were invited to 'The Grand Ball'. Ella got treated so badly by the other girls! When she made her beautiful dress to wear to the ball, Jezela and Annastagia ripped it! When they arrived at the ball Jezela and Anastasia were wearing sparkling gowns and Ella was wearing rags. Prince Charming saw Ella and stared... 'I want her as my wife!' he announced! Ella was embarrassed and ran down a flight of stairs. Oh no! She slipped! The Prince thought there was only one thing to do... 'I must kiss her!' Ella came back to life.

Esmé Nancy Allen (10)
Ridgeway Middle School, Redditch

Snow White And The Seven Dwarfs

Snow White's father had just wed and he was happy, but Snow White felt a little left out and jealous of the attention her stepmother got. Her stepmother was jealous of her, she asked her mirror who was prettiest, it always said Snow. Her stepmother got so jealous she ordered a huntsman to rip out her heart and he did but she carried on living. She got so very angry that she got seven dwarfs to comb Snow White's lovely hair with poisoned combs and fed her lots and lots of perfectly healthy looking poisoned apples until she slept forever.

Kamesha Agyarko (10)
Ridgeway Middle School, Redditch

The Goblin's Story

Once upon a time there lived three dwarfs called Melb, Jelb and Belb. They got loads of materials then started to build a house, but Astonugly did not like this so she grabbed her magic stick and said, 'No more, this is mine and none of yours.' Fortunately, she knocked two of the brilliant houses, went to the brick house and did her strongest spell – *crash!* She kept the kind little dwarfs as slaves, and turned them into horrid, nasty, fat goblins. She laughed and laughed, they were pink, blue and green. She was the evil witch after all!

Holly Neal (10)
Ridgeway Middle School, Redditch

Sleeping Beauty

Once upon a time, there lived a wealthy king and queen who longed to have a baby girl. One day the queen gave birth to a girl, they were so delighted that they invited all the fairies in the kingdom to celebrate. Just then the doors swung open and in flew Maleficent... Now she was not that bad, in fact she was so thrilled, she cast a spell on Aurora! On her sixteenth birthday the spell came true. Aurora spent all her days in the meadows for one hundred years until one day she married and was locked up forever...

Storm Cox (10)
Ridgeway Middle School, Redditch

Little Red Riding Hood

Once upon a time there was a little girl named Little Red Riding Hood. She was on her weekly stroll in the wood and suddenly she fell into a ditch and Little Red Riding Hood broke her legs and then her left eye popped out! Sadly a wolf showed up and ate her in one giant mouthful. The red hooded figure was no more. Granny came along and karate-chopped the wolf in half! The local woodcutter appeared and cut off Granny's head! Sadly he tripped and drowned in the nearby pond! They all lived sadly ever after.

Oliver Cooke (10)
Ridgeway Middle School, Redditch

Gretel And Hansel

Once upon a time two children named Hansel and Gretel had an adventure. They were living with their wicked uncle. One night they took a walk to stay up late. After walking for about fifteen minutes they saw a figure. 'I'll make loads of money with this watch,' he exclaimed. So Hansel called the police and they came and arrested him. He was put on trial and the judge sentenced him to ten years in the freezer. The gingerbread house the thief was living in was sold on eBay and Hansel and Gretel got a massive house as their reward.

Toby Reading (10)
Ridgeway Middle School, Redditch

The Little Pink Pig

Once upon a time, in a not very far away village, lived a dragon called Agnus, a giant called Timbra, a pig called Gloria and last but by no means least, a child called Sheila. Timbra gave a tray full of fabrics for Sheila to take to Gloria, her grandma. She took the path and met a dragon, he was nice. They arrived, the dragon turned bad, ate them all, and shrunk. Then they went time travelling to lots of historical sites. When they got back, Timbra and Agnus were married! Unfortunately, Gloria died. They ate her for their Christmas dinner.

Isabella Crellin (10)
Ridgeway Middle School, Redditch

The Bad Wizard

Once upon a time there was a boy called Charlie who went out to play. On the way he saw a friendly looking wizard who he went to speak to. The wizard asked him whether he wanted to go to his house for lunch and Charlie said, 'Yes please.'
When they arrived the wizard took out his wand and turned poor Charlie into a frog. He went to find help but everybody avoided him. A kind fairy saw that he needed help so turned him back to his normal form and then turned the wizard into a frog.

Evan Miles (11)
Ridgeway Middle School, Redditch

The Little Witch

One stormy night Claudia Little Witch was up to her spells. Claudia had no friends because she was different. They made fun of her clothes, they made fun of her parents, they even made fun of her dog. One night, Claudia got so angry she decided to use magic to curse the other children, whether they were being mean or not! The next morning everyone was being even more mean. At lunch a new girl came, her name was Jasmine. Claudia wanted a new friend, so her and Jasmine were best friends.
Never bully people who are different!

Lily Sofia Onions (11)
Ridgeway Middle School, Redditch

The Three Little Pigs (Silly Edition)

The wolf had blown the house of sticks down. The two pigs ran to their brother's house made of bricks. When they got there the house was made of flowers! The pigs went inside, the wolf marched to the door and yelled, 'That's not how the story goes, you're meant to use bricks.'
'Bob the builder needed them,' whimpered the pig.
'Get more bricks!' he yelled. The pigs got the bricks and built the house, the wolf tried to blow it down, he couldn't. Wolf angrily shouted, 'Right, that does it, where's Little Red Riding Hood, maybe I'll eat her.'

Kathryn Taylor (11)
Ridgeway Middle School, Redditch

Goldilocks And The Four Bears

Once upon a time there were four bears, they lived in a big forest and in that forest was a little cottage and in that cottage lived the bears. One day they went in search of some berries. Just as they left, Daddy Bear turned on the security system. Then left too. A girl called Goldilocks came along and saw the cottage and went in. She accidentally set off the alarm and a wrecking ball came and destroyed the little cottage. When the four bears came back they were so mad they made Goldilocks their slave forever.

Charlotte Flower (10)
Ridgeway Middle School, Redditch

Cinderella

Once lived Cinderella in a small town. She worked for her evil stepmother and her two stepsisters. They were cruel and fancy, each of them.

One day Cinderella went on an accessories shop to Topshop and saw the prince there. They fell madly in love. The prince held a royal ball in order to see Cinderella. Every lady was to attend, and again they met. But when Luke (the prince) was proposing, Cinderella sighed and said, 'No thank you, I'd rather be single. But you could give me a job.' Which he did, she was now his hairdresser.

Maddie Gregory (10)
Ridgeway Middle School, Redditch

Little Red Riding Hood

Once upon a time there was a girl called Little Red Riding Hood. On one misty cold day she was told by her mother to go to her gran's house and take some food for her. On the way to her gran's house, she saw a wolf, and when he wasn't looking, she jumped on him, scared him, and ran away laughing and giggling. The wolf got angry so he decided to follow Little Red Riding Hood to her gran's house. She ran inside the house, leaving the wolf all alone outside. Suddenly the gran came out and stabbed him!

Jasmine Frost (10)
Ridgeway Middle School, Redditch

A Magical Fairy Tale

Once upon a time there was a girl called Sophie, she had long brown hair. One day she decided to read a book: 'Fairy Tales Forever'. Suddenly the pages started flickering. *Whoosh!* A fairy godmother was standing right in front of her. 'This can't be real, fairy tales aren't true!' said Sophie.
'They are if you believe.' Suddenly the fairy godmother waved her wand and *bang!* Sophie had a long blue and purple dress. 'You shall believe in fairy tales!'
Sophie smiled, 'Thank you...' The fairy godmother was gone.
Sophie had the best day and always believed in fairy tales.

Maeve Winn (10)
Ridgeway Middle School, Redditch

The Pirate

Once upon a time there lived a pirate called Billy. One day he decided to go on a sailing trip, but once he had got out to sea, a storm came and washed the boat away! When he awoke he didn't know where he was, then he heard a massive roar! Billy didn't know what to do... Billy started to run, Billy was startled from the noise and he knew there was danger on the island. Then a gigantic T-rex came from out of the blue, he panicked but all he could say was, 'That's the best thing ever!'

Harvey Sharpe (11)
Ridgeway Middle School, Redditch

The Lion And The Rabbit!

Once upon a time there was a lion who thought he was the bravest, brightest and best, well he pretended, he was just lazy and scared. One day a rabbit came along and said, 'Hello, how are you today?' And the lion just grunted.
'What is wrong?'
'I just wish I was the bravest and the best because I'm not really, I just pretend.'
'Well, maybe I can help. If I can't there's a dog who can help.'
'OK, when do we start?'
'Now!'
So they went to go and see Dog and then he got braver.

Georgia Wright (11)
Ridgeway Middle School, Redditch

The Book

Once upon a time there was a girl and her mum used to always read her a bedtime story. The phone rang one night so the mum went to get it while the girl tried reading the book herself. Suddenly she got sucked into the book. She walked into the land and stared, she saw Humpty Dumpty and loads more characters. The wolf was in the wood looking for a tasty meal: the pigs! So he went and ate them up. The girl heard her mum's footsteps so she got out of the book and that's it.

India Macvie (11)
Ridgeway Middle School, Redditch

The Beginning By Einstein The Hamster

I met my owner one Saturday morning in February 2015, he was looking through the hamster cages. I didn't know he was looking through because I was asleep in my bare little cage. I knew it was being cleaned out. Day by day no one wanted me. I was near going to the rescue home and would never get an owner. My fortune was to change when a hand smacked me out of the cage and put me in a box. I went into another box and was taken over to the tills, outside and into the car, happy.

Quinn Arthur Mason-Burke (11)
Ridgeway Middle School, Redditch

Toy Story 10

One day, in California, there was a boy called Matthew. He lived in Home Lane, he was getting ready for school and his friend came over and he came in and suddenly a portal appeared and Matt fell in. He started to turn into plastic, he was in Andy's room and all of his toys were alive. One of them greeted him, he was scared but happy at the same time. He went to the other toys and played for a bit until it was time to go.

Tyler Tillsley (10)
Ridgeway Middle School, Redditch

Bob Saves The Day

Once upon a time there was a guinea pig. He was just a normal guinea pig. Most of his friends were heroes like Bob, he became a hero because he got manager of the day, anyway, his job was a rainbow drop collector. Basically, you just go round the rainbow and collect drops.

One day he caught someone sneaking around the restricted area in the bush. He crept over there and saw a man getting rainbow drops. He hid and shouted, 'Get out!' He stayed still so Bob jumped on him and he fell over and Bob became a hero.

Alex Matthew Taylor (12)
Ridgeway Middle School, Redditch

The Marriage

In Canada, at the church in the sky, Little Red Riding Hood was going to get married to Jack. Suddenly the wolf gobbled them down. Just then the wolf fell out of the sky in a basket. He fell on the rough and hard ground. One minute later Jack picked them out slowly, they got out of his mouth and got a spiky iron bat and sliced him. They were late for their wedding. They got there in time. It was time to go inside. Red put on the golden ring and nicely kissed the lovely boy.

Tyler Carter (11)
Ridgeway Middle School, Redditch

Dolly

Once upon a time there was a little girl called Megan. When she was little she dropped her dolly down the stairs. Every year on the 12th of June a doll called Dolly haunted her in her dreams. That night Megan saw Dolly in her dream but she saw a book under her bed. It was gold and brown. It opened up and landed on a particular page. It said bye-bye Dolly, so Megan read out the song, 'Voo, voo, la, la, la, bye-bye Dolly, go away Dolly.' After that Dolly was never seen again in her dreams.

Izzy Street (10)
Ridgeway Middle School, Redditch

Spots

Once upon a time there was a horse called Ellie. In her barn all her friends teased her because she was different. Elile's dream was to be spotless.
One day she was wondering why she couldn't be normal then Maddie came. 'What are you doing sitting there?' she asked.
'See you later, little Miss Spots.'
Then Milly came and said, 'There is a way you know, the famous cream bush, just put some on.' She did. No one recognised her but when she woke the spots were back. Surprisingly, all her friends had spots too. She was like the others.

Sophie Olivia Newman (10)
Ridgeway Middle School, Redditch

The House King

Once upon a time there was a man called Billy. He bought a haunted house, but little did he know what lived there. The doors just opened by themselves, something spooky was going on. Billy walked into the house and he heard some strange noises. He looked around and saw some strange looking creatures. They started chasing Billy around the house. Then Billy fell over, but he managed to get up. He hid in a closet and jumped out and scared the creatures and they all disappeared into dust, never to be seen again.

Billy Brind (10)
Ridgeway Middle School, Redditch

Jack And Cinderella

Once upon a time there was a boy who lived with his mother. One day the boy found some beans. He took the beans to his friend's house, he wasn't there so he took them to his mum. She said, 'Great, we can have something else for dinner tonight.'
The next day the boy woke and he heard a girl singing, he was full from eating his beans. He went over to the girl and said, 'Do you like beans?'
She replied, 'Beans give me dreams.' The boy gave her some beans, she became the girl of his dreams.

Nadine Louise Westerman (11)
Ridgeway Middle School, Redditch

The Haunted Castle

Once upon a time in the deep, dark woods there was a haunted castle. A boy called Dan went to see who was living there. When he opened the door it squeaked loudly. Inside was a bat, his name was Mr Bat. 'Let me show you around,' he said.
'Thank you,' said Dan.
'Let's go.' They went off. On their way there they saw Mr Monster and Mr Ghost. 'Oh I forgot to tell you Dan, there are lots of traps in this castle,' said Mr Bat.
'Quickly, to the chamber room, let's save Dan.'
'It's too late!'

Aidan Paul Baker (10)
Ridgeway Middle School, Redditch

The Dangerous World

Once upon a time there were these brave humans (soldiers). The main soldier was called Billy. One day when the soldiers were training, suddenly these aliens came and ghosts and they said their captains' names... Bob and Jeff. They said they were going to take over the world. Our soldiers tried to stop them. The battle went on for more than two years. Finally, after two years, the aliens and ghosts won.

Max Laband (10)
Ridgeway Middle School, Redditch

Ghosts

In a village in the middle of lots of fields there are three miles of fields and this village. Every night people would hear really scary noises that would make them look everywhere for ghosts. There were loads of ghosts...
One night a woman heard a weird sound that sounded like a robber was downstairs. She went downstairs and nothing was there. Suddenly, the mirror fell off the wall and smashed on her foot, then she heard a faint voice say, 'Go back to bed now.' She got scared and ran off to bed and hid.

Finley Browning (10)
Ridgeway Middle School, Redditch

Friendship Trouble

Once upon a time, Wasibi Warriors and Ballet Studio met in one room and taught their partners what they knew. The leaders said Wasibi Warriors and Ballet Studio couldn't be BFFs so they needed to keep that a secret, and their boyfriends a secret.
One day they were engaged by the evil Maleficent who cursed the ring and it could kill them all...
Kim and Jack were married and Lylia and Jacob were married too. After, their kids found out that the rings were cursed by Maleficent so they threw them away so everything was happy...

Emilia Betteridge (10)
Ridgeway Middle School, Redditch

Submarine Saga

Once upon a time there were two boys called Jack and Ed, they stole a submarine and off they went. Suddenly, the submarine sank and banged into... a shark! It tried to get in and a zombie got in and bit Ed. Happily, they got to shore, luckily there was a bus that took them to the hospital. Ed was okay now, so off they went to defeat the witch and she died.

Conor Jack Lester (10)
Ridgeway Middle School, Redditch

The Story Of True Love

Once upon a time there was a princess called Bella, she lived in a village with her dad. A prince called Harry lived with his mom. She was a witch but he did not know. Harry wanted to get married but he could not find a girl. His mom did not want him to get married. He set off. He knocked on the door, Bella came. The witch was doing magic poison to make her young. She made up a name called Sienna. Harry thought Bella was the one and the witch did not bite Harry. They got married.

Jess Badsey (10)
Ridgeway Middle School, Redditch

Zombie Invasion

Once upon a time there were two boys, Bill and Tyler, and their dog Fang. They were friends. One day they were playing a game in the library and they met George. They became friends but just then a zombie came in and bit the librarian. They jumped out of the window and ran to Tyler's hideout (nobody knows about) and they went out to see what was there. They saw a witch and she was making more zombies. Then Bill hugged Fang and then one zombie vanished and they saved the Earth and humanity with the power of love.

Tyler Smith (10)
Ridgeway Middle School, Redditch

People Vs Monsters!

One day there were three people called Rick, Carl and Jess who were wandering in the woods and they saw an asylum. They looked at it for a minute and were sucked into the asylum. They were stuck. They all felt a chill and then they found out the asylum was haunted. They got their weapons out ready. They got their swords and crossbows out and they were armed. They saw a lever and pulled it and they were free. They got back to their families and lived happily ever after. However, the mansion was still there...

Tom Partridge (10)
Ridgeway Middle School, Redditch

It's A Scary Story

Once upon a time lived two girls, one of them was called Princess Rosalina and the other one was called Lily. She was not a princess. Lily lived in a haunted house but she didn't know and Princess Rosalina lived in a haunted castle but didn't know either. Rosalina lived in an underwater world and strange things were happening like goblins in their gardens. Finally they met up with each other and went to the park at midnight, where they heard a scream and Lily got shot... They didn't live happily ever after!

Ellie Cooper (10)
Ridgeway Middle School, Redditch

Pet Wars!

Once upon a time there was a planet called Maboo. On the planet there was the pet order. The pet order was under attack by the frost legion. In the battle the hamster troops were fighting the evil snowmen. Two Jedi cats called Anakin Catwalker and Obi-Wan Kitty duelled the emperor snowman and won. A team of ninja dogs killed all the frost legion troops. After that the pet order lived in peace and the frost legion were no more. The planet Maboo was safe.

Jasper Harman (10)
Ridgeway Middle School, Redditch

The Cinderella Story With A Twist

Once upon a time there was a little girl who loved her father, the girl's name was Ella. Ella's birthday came. Weirdly her father had his eyes on a woman. Ella's father spent loads of time with this woman, they got married. Ella's father told Ella that he loved her. Suddenly the house shook, there it was, an earthquake. Ella had a lucky escape, however Ella's father was unlucky.
Ten years later, the time for the high school prom came and Ella was asked by the sweetest boy. After the prom Ella found out she liked him and he liked her.

Hibba Razzak (10)
Ridgeway Middle School, Redditch

Pigs Meet The Turkey

Once upon a time there were three pigs: Pork, Sausage and Bacon. Pork was the oldest and cleverest, whereas Sausage was very dumb and the youngest. Bacon was calm and clever. Today they'd move out of their house and build their own. Pork built his house out of concrete, Sausage built his out of potatoes and Bacon built his out of chocolate.
After a week the turkey knew they lived there and squashed Bacon's house, then he went to Sausage's house but he wasn't there because he was at Pork's house eating cake and having fun, very safe and comfortable.

Abbie Mae Morland (10)
Ridgeway Middle School, Redditch

Goldilocks And The Three Evil Bears

Once upon a time there were three evil bears. The bears went to visit the witch across the forest. While the bears were out they had an intruder, Goldilocks. She sat gracefully in Daddy Bear's chair. It was uncomfy, she sat on Baby's chair, it collapsed. She left the porridge and ran upstairs. She felt sleepy. She lay on Mama Bear's bed, it was comfy. After she slept the mum came and woke her up. The bears were staring. Mama Bear grabbed Goldilocks and threw her out of the glass window, and they all laughed.

Lauren Mernagh (10)
Ridgeway Middle School, Redditch

Lisa, The Whale And Dolphin

Once upon a time there was a little girl called Lisa. She lived in a street called The Ocean. Lisa was only 11 years old. Lisa walked to the beach because she had an argument with her friend and boyfriend. Lisa jumped into the sea. She loved it there. She thought she was dreaming for an hour or two. Lisa saw a magic witch. She turned Lisa into a mermaid with powers. The fish swam away from her. She met the whale and dolphin, they made best friends and they lived happily ever after forever and ever.

Fiona Rodgers (11)
Ridgeway Middle School, Redditch

Gnome Love

Once upon a time there was a lady called Mrs Gnome, her house was in the woods. Her house was horrible but she lived by herself. She was very lonely. One day she went outside for a walk. Suddenly, she fell over and hurt her ankle, she shouted for help. Mr Gnome ran over there and looked after her. He took her to his house. They fell in love and lived together in the woods. The spell was broken and her house looked beautiful again.

Kameron Oliver (11)
Ridgeway Middle School, Redditch

The Alien Invasion

On a beach, in the middle of the hottest summer ever, Ronaldo, Messi, Iniesta and Wilshaw were playing football on the beach and having a good time. Suddenly they saw a huge silver thing in the sky. 'It's aliens,' shouted Iniesta. The aliens were not scared of Messi and Ronaldo but they were scared of Iniesta and Wilshaw. The green ugly aliens invaded the whole town. They destroyed most of the old, minging town. Then, in the corner of Messi's eye, he saw an alien crying. He went over to see what was the matter. Alien said, 'I am hurt!'

Taylor Flemming (11)
Ridgeway Middle School, Redditch

Untitled

Once upon a time there was a girl called Little Red Riding Hood. After what happened with the whole wolf situation, she wasn't very happy, so she thought she should take revenge on the wolf. She waited in the woods for the wolf to appear.

In the morning she woke up and saw the wolf walking on the path. She asked the wolf where he was going.

'I am going to visit my grandma,' the wolf replied.

She ran straight to his grandma's house and gobbled her up. When the wolf came she gobbled him up too!

George Joseph Hall (10)
Ridgeway Middle School, Redditch

Red Riding Hood With A Twist

Once upon a time there was a girl named Red Riding Hood, as you can guess there is a reason for her to wear a hood. Let me tell you the story...

One night, with not a person in sight, a red figure appeared, it dashed into the shop and came out with a full potato sack, then the window smashed and the alarm went off. The police came and grabbed her and threw her in jail. The police officer looked up, it was Granny and now they were running away.

Daisy Fear (10)
Ridgeway Middle School, Redditch

Untitled

Once upon a time there were two cities, one was good and one was bad. One was underwater and one was on land. They needed to build an underwater city, but they were under attack. City 1's army was attacking the underwater base because they didn't like the underwater base. Super Ben and Clayton saved the underwater base but they had to fall back to the city. The bad city followed Super Ben and Clayton to their city and the bad people attacked. However, a whale came to save Ben and Clayton.

Benjamin Head (11)
Ridgeway Middle School, Redditch

Untitled

Once upon a time there were three heroes, they created a city to live on but they did not know they'd built it next to a bad city who killed whoever lived next to them. If they didn't move they would die... The fish people knew what was going to happen but they refused. They wouldn't stand up to the bad city but the three heroes knew what to do. They needed weapons, they needed to build a shield so they said, 'Let's build this.'
They were building the biggest base but the bad guys came anyway...

Ben Brian Ticer (11)
Ridgeway Middle School, Redditch

Sleepover Fun!

Kyra, Megan, Jade and Kamesha are quadruplets. They have BFFs called Elia and Lilly.
One day Elia and Lilly went to their house, they decided to go into the living room where they chatted about what they were going to do. They decided to play hide-and-seek. Eventually Elia had found everybody, except Lilly. They shouted Lilly but there was no answer. They started to become worried. They checked everywhere, there was no sign of her. Suddenly, they heard a noise in the kitchen, Lilly was stuck in the washing machine. They called their parents and eventually she was out.

Kyra Rice (10)
Ridgeway Middle School, Redditch

Bunny Palaver

One sunny day, Ellie was watering her flowers and playing with her rabbits. Every day Ellie would love to water her flowers and play with her rabbits. They were called Snowy and Woolly, Ellie loved them. The rabbits were out running for ages. Ellie finally went looking for them. She couldn't find them so she called her friend so they could help. They did. They searched and searched for hours and hours and finally found them. Ellie looked at Snowy and said, 'She's pregnant.' They soon had five new bunnies wandering round and Ellie loved it.

Ellisia Heel (10)
Ridgeway Middle School, Redditch

The Honeycomb Story

A long time ago there lived a unicorn called Moses. Moses had recently eaten a honeycomb and got sticky in his tummy button. So he called his friend Squiddle the squirrel and Squibble the squidnugget tried to pop the honey out. They tried to squeeze it out but it would not budge. In the end Moses could not get it out so he had a cup of tea and spilt the cup of tea. It melted away the honey so they decided to have an awkward dance party. The end at last.

Leah Share (10)
Ridgeway Middle School, Redditch

The Trick!

There was a menacing boy called Callum and he had a little sister called Charlotte and Callum always used to play tricks on her. One day Callum walked into the bathroom and he put gum everywhere. Then about five minutes later Charlotte walked into the bathroom to wash her hands because she was cooking. Charlotte stepped into the bathroom and screamed, 'Callum!' Then she started to cry. About a second later Mom came in. She said, 'Stop being horrible.' She said, 'Get to your room,' so Callum went to his room and suddenly he said, 'I've got a good idea.'...

Nathan Philip Stephen Bennett (10)
Ridgeway Middle School, Redditch

Matt's Time Machine

One Saturday morning Matt Jr finished his time machine. He tested the machine, it worked like a charm.

The next morning he wrote a letter saying he went through. As soon as he got out a giant foot stomped on the machine. He was in dinosaur times. Because he was a smart kid he thought, *first I have to build a shelter and get weapons and food.*

Fifteen years later Matt Jr built the machine to go back and forth to see his dinosaur friends called Dave and Fred.

Matthew Kennedy (10)
Ridgeway Middle School, Redditch

Holly's Missing Diary

There was a girl called Holly, and she had always written in her diary about wanting a puppy, but now she has one and her name is Poppy!

The next beautiful day Holly wanted to write in her diary but it was gone! Holly looked everywhere until she finally saw Poppy with it in bed. Holly's diary was pink so was Poppy's bed, so it would have been hard to find it. Anyway, Holly was very scared but she finally found it just before bedtime. Holly went to bed and dreamed about her amazing day and what she did.

Iyesha Latoya Campbell (10)
Ridgeway Middle School, Redditch

75

Shrek And The Gold

One day there was a man called Shrek. He lived in a house with his wife and pet monkey. There was one person called Bad Gold who stole all of the gold and they were poor. Shrek needed to do something so he came up with a plan. He would get Bad Gold to run into the trap he set. He came running... 'You're trapped.' A couple of minutes later Shrek came to the trap and got all the money back. When he got the money he shared it and they lived with their money that they had.

Samuel William Humphray (10)
Ridgeway Middle School, Redditch

The Good/bad Knight

There was a knight who was valiant called Jeff the Great. Their king was angry because Amy went missing. Jeff saw a dragon with a girl. Every time he shot his arrow from a bow and arrow he missed. He made a lot of potion, I mean a lot, he loved her so much he would die for her. He went out and threw loads of potions at the dragon but he missed and hit himself. It turned out Amy was just riding it and now Jeff the Great is a bad knight!

Ross Alan Parkinson (10)
Ridgeway Middle School, Redditch

The Dolphin's Day

It was a lovely day, there was a dolphin who was called Jerry, the main dolphin. He was a baby dolphin, he had blue eyes and a mom and dad who both had blue mouths. One day Jerry went off on his own and had a little swim. He came to a very new addition in the bottom of the wavy ocean. It was really weird. There was a very big piece of an old boat that was rusty, mangled and ginormous. So he wormed his way around the boat. He looked... it was really big.

Amey Martin (10)
Ridgeway Middle School, Redditch

Mr Porkchop And The Aliens

Mr Porkchop, a pig, lived on a farm. He liked to eat carrots and potatoes and playing with his friends Coco the cat and Dave the dog. One day before he went to bed, he heard a crash in his garden. He called his friends to come and see what it was, it looked like a spaceship that crashed. They went outside and found four aliens Bing, Bong, Bang and Beng. Mr Porkchop and his friends called up scientist Alfie the sheep. When he arrived the spaceship had disappeared, leaving Squidnuggets. The animals, still shocked, enjoyed the snack.

Tegan Kocker (10)
Ridgeway Middle School, Redditch

Saving The World

There once was a girl who lived in a village, her name was Izzy. She was really good at karate. Meanwhile Dr Evil was in his lab. Dr Evil was a mad man. He wanted to take over the world. He finally had a master plan. Izzy spotted a spacecraft, it was Doctor Evil's. He stepped out from his spacecraft. 'I'm here to destroy you!' he shouted. Izzy and Doctor Evil were fighting for what seemed like forever. Finally, Doctor Evil was defeated for good. Izzy could now go back to being a normal yet talented little girl.

Jessica Wedgbury (10)
Ridgeway Middle School, Redditch

Untitled

Ender was curious enough to walk through a tree. When he walked through he found himself in a world he couldn't explain. 'Is this true? I'm saved!' said a man from behind. He said his name was Martyn and that he needed help escaping this world. He took Ender to this cave that had a portal-like structure. He needed to turn it on, there was a beep in the wall. A device stuck out of it. He pulled it out. It said a lightning bolt was going to hit the portal. The lightning hit and the portal opened...

Ashton Neil Brown (11)
Ridgeway Middle School, Redditch

The Naughty Girl

There was once a little boy called Steve, he had a sister called Sophie. She was always naughty. When Steve went to bed, Sophie left a cup of cold water by him in the night. Sometimes she would even jump out of the window. One day she went too far, she went to the police and played a trick. She went to the boss and said that people were breaking her aunty's windows. The boss ran to the phone and ran to the rescue. When Boss got back he shouted as loud as he could. Sophie got grounded.

Samuel Whelan (9)
Ridgeway Middle School, Redditch

The Big Match

Today it was the FA Cup Final, Villa Vs WBA. The players arrived at Wembley. They got changed into their kits and lined up in the tunnel, they were jumping up and down. The fans were screaming and shouting. It was Villa Vs WBA. They were passing the ball around like crazy. Suddenly Delph played a through ball to Benteke. He shot and scored! What a finish – 1-0. Villa were surely on the road to win the cup. It would have been 3 decades since they won it! So Aston Villa won the FA Cup 1-0!

Harvey George Saunders (10)
Ridgeway Middle School, Redditch

The Football Showdown

Today it was the big final of Manchester Vs Arsenal. Just before it was on live Harrison was estimating who would win. He guessed Manchester would score two and Arsenal would score four. The match came on minutes later. Harrison was hyper. Arsenal were his favourite team, that's why he wanted them to score. The game was playing when suddenly a player named Sanchez got injured and there was no substitution to cover for him. Then this man named Benj sprinted onto the pitch and said, 'I'll play for Sanchez.' The Arsenal manager said, 'OK,' and then Arsenal won.

Ryan Welsh (11)
Ridgeway Middle School, Redditch

The Chocolate Thief!

There was a cottage in the middle of a big forest, filled with chocolate.
One day a monkey called Milo was walking and found the cottage, he discovered the door. Milo tiptoed inside. He looked down, there were chocolate crumbs. Milo decided to follow them, they led to a cupboard. He poked his head in the cupboard, there was a huge mountain of chocolate! Every day Milo came back and ate it. He ate so much he was stuck in the cupboard. Milo looked around, there was butter. He smothered it all over himself. Milo pushed and slipped out!

Hollie May Tapscott (10)
Ridgeway Middle School, Redditch

The Beast

As I carefully opened the broken, woody door I saw a disturbing figure's shadow. I heard his nose twitching, it was getting louder. He was getting closer... Panicking I ran out of my house to the beach where I was sure he wouldn't find me. After what seemed like hours, I finally headed home to my air-conditioned house. I climbed through the little window of my bedroom and felt a gush of cold air hit me. Finally I was out of the boiling sun... Once again I saw the shadow of the beast! But I also saw him as my pet.

Sam Padfield (10)
Ridgeway Middle School, Redditch

Sprinkles

There's a planet 3,906 miles from Earth. It's a giant doughnut with sprinkles living on it. Some of them are Midge the baby, also the hero of the story, Mouldy the elder sprinkle and Choco the chocolate frog. The evil one!
It was a normal peaceful day on Doughnut Planet until... Choco the frog came! He came to eat the planet until Midge came to stop Choco. He laughed at Midge because she was a baby and said she couldn't fight him! But he was wrong, he didn't know Midge knew karate. She defeated him with one huge, almighty kick!

Issie D'Albert (10)
Ridgeway Middle School, Redditch

Evacuees' Life

I'm scared, I don't know what's going to happen. As I walk, long greens brush against my legs. I squeeze tightly to my mother's hand, while wetness runs down my face. I stand and wait for the train to come. I get on and wave goodbye as the train puffs away. Crying all the way my friends keep me company. I don't know what to do. I feel so alone, even though my whole school is with me. When I arrive I walk to a school. One by one adults take us to their homes. I feel all alone...

Megan Jessie June Haines (11)
Ridgeway Middle School, Redditch

We're In The Jungle!

Me and my friends walked through the vines and trees excitedly. Suddenly we heard a big loud roar. We followed the sound as it got louder. Suddenly a lion jumped out of the bushes. We ran as fast as we could until we lost it.
We took pictures of the colourful parrots singing sweetly. 'This is amazing!' shouted Alara.
'Yes, like the best day ever!' added Courtney.
'Let's go and find a picnic spot,' said Tali. So we all went and had a lovely picnic. Soon it was time to go.

Tali Allyssia Perry (10)
Ridgeway Middle School, Redditch

The Pig Who Could Fly

One sunny day there was a pig and he saw a beautiful butterfly, he thought hard then said he wanted to fly. Everyone else just laughed at him. Mr Pig was very sad.

The next day he rolled in the stinky mud and loads of flies were attracted to the smell. They got stuck to Mr Pig and tried to fly but they were stuck, but they eventually flew Mr Pig with them. He was so happy.

Faith Holtom (10)
Ridgeway Middle School, Redditch

Stuck In The Car

I awoke. I was confused, how could I be in front of a steering wheel? I looked out of the frosty window. I saw people walking past in woolly jackets. I started banging on the cold window but nobody could hear me so I started shouting, 'Help.' Then the car started moving. It kept going up and up into the sky. My heart started pounding fast so I shouted, 'Stop!' The car suddenly froze in mid-air. I caught a glimpse out of the corner of my eye, who was that on the back seat?

Jessica Prosser (10)
Ridgeway Middle School, Redditch

The Naughty Frog

'Another day in Chocolate Land with that naughty frog stealing all the chocolate!' moaned the chocolate pig. Now the pig did not like the frog taking all his chocolate. The horse on the other hand just gave him some. The pig was very, very unkind to the frog, and never shared a thing with him so the frog just stole, he knew it was naughty but he did it mostly for fun, and then ate it all. 'Om, nom!' he would say. The horse was a very, very kind chocolate horse and would share all his food with the frog.

Lucy Stringer (10)
Ridgeway Middle School, Redditch

The Countryside

As I got to the train station I waved bye to my mom, it was the saddest time of my life. I saw my friend Esme sitting down by herself so I went over to cheer her up. We chatted for a while then the train came. We hopped onboard the train. When we got to the countryside there was an empty hall. We went inside the hall, and there were masses of adults waiting to adopt us. Then all of a sudden somebody came up to me and said, 'Come home with me,' so I did.

Katelin Partridge (10)
Ridgeway Middle School, Redditch

My Evacuee Sister

Just arriving at the train station was heartbreaking enough. Seeing my sister get on that evacuation train, and not being able to go with her, was devastating. The day before we packed her case, clothes were everywhere. We did everything together that day and even tried to help Mum. Mum cooked hers and Elizabeth's favourite pasta... Then the train was gone. It only took 15 minutes to get there. The next week I got a letter, it read 'Dear Texas, I'm here'... I couldn't read any more, it was too hard. I missed her.

Emily Wright (11)
Ridgeway Middle School, Redditch

Exploring Planet Earth Today

Courtney and Tali were out exploring, Charlie and Joe were chasing cheetahs, Jack and Reece were exploring the jungle like they always do and I was doing maths. It was 8.30pm so we went in to do some jobs like researching facts about all the things that we found, we all had something to eat that night then we all went to bed.
In the morning we all had breakfast. Then we all went exploring, even me. No maths for me today, I really wanted to do maths today but my friends wanted me to go exploring so I did.

Spencer Ryan Ellis (10)
Ridgeway Middle School, Redditch

The Day Of Awakening!

This morning I woke at a blink of an eye. As I sprung out of bed I realised it was 8.40, I said to myself, 'Oh no, I am so late!' I rushed to get dressed, I was now even later, therefore I hurried out the door and ran as fast as a cheetah to the Pokémon centre. Once I had arrived I met Professor Sycamore at the door, he greeted me with my Pokémon Eevee! After he had told me about Eevee inside he handed me a Pokédex to find out about different Pokémon. Eevee and I ran home!

Jack Peter William Povey (10)
Ridgeway Middle School, Redditch

The Elephant Stuck In The Fridge

Once there was an elephant who was in the kitchen to get some peanuts. But his little brother, Small Elephant, bumped into the fridge elephant was at and he got stuck! When Mummy Kitten came to get carrots out of the fridge she said, 'How did you do that?' So Mummy Kitten said she would call the fire dog. All kinds of spreads and jams came to help, but in the end the thing that worked was peanut butter! 'Thank you!' the elephant exclaimed.

Caitlin Williams (10)
Ridgeway Middle School, Redditch

The Giraffe Who Wanted To Become A Famous Animal Runner And Jumper

There once was a giraffe named Vanessa. The next day she gave birth to a beautiful baby boy. She named him Oscar. From the age of two Oscar wanted to become a famous animal runner and jumper. When Oscar was four he went down to the riverbank to jump the river. He ran and got his front paws to the bank but his back legs got the best of him and Oscar landed in the river with a splash. After weeks of training he finally made it to the other side. He thought how to get back over...

Scarlett R J Seymour (10)
Ridgeway Middle School, Redditch

Untitled

There was a little girl called Little Red Riding Hood who went to deliver some muffins to her grandma but she didn't know there was someone at Grandma's house. When she got there she saw the wolf cooking something in the kitchen so she went in and chased the wolf around the house. When her grandma came back from picking berries she explained that the wolf was a friend.

Dillon Williams
Ridgeway Middle School, Redditch

The Three Little Pigs

Once upon a time there were three little pigs who built their houses in the woods. One built their house out of leaves, one built their house out of sticks and the other made it out of bricks. A wolf tried to blow it down but a unicorn came and put a magic bubble around it that only the pigs could get through, but the wolf tried to eat them when they went out. The unicorn put a bubble around the three little pigs. The wolf never tried to annoy the three little pigs again. They lived happily ever after.

Rebecca Louise Cole (11)
Ridgeway Middle School, Redditch

The Sheep Who Loved Custard

Once there was a sheep who loved custard, he went to go get some when he bumped into a witch who asked, 'What are you doing here?'
The sheep said, 'I'm getting some custard.'
The witch smiled and said, 'I have some, you can come with me to get some.'
'Sure,' the sheep replied. He was happy so he hopped on her broom and went to her cottage. 'You're my tea now!' The sheep was crying for help then a man came by and stopped the witch and she ran off. The sheep had learnt not to trust strangers.

Olivia Cherry (11)
Ridgeway Middle School, Redditch

Little Blue Britney

Once upon a time a little bright blue girl turned up at her grandmother's house, just to check up on her. When she opened the door she saw a wolf eating her grandma. Suddenly the wolf noticed her and took one large bite and she was already in his belly. The wolf laughed to himself, 'Ha, ha!'
In came a local axeman and said, 'Is it done? Are they gone?'
'Yes,' replied the wolf.
The axeman paid the wolf and the wolf was never to be seen again. The axeman lived happily ever after in the house.

Jack Wright (11)
Ridgeway Middle School, Redditch

Magical Man

Once upon a time there was a man with all the magical powers he could have wanted. Because of his powers and abilities he obviously lived in a castle with servants and everything. All of the villagers thought he was a very nice and generous guy, but he had a dark side. When he was younger, without the castle, he wanted to show the villagers his magic tricks, but they failed and all of the villagers laughed at him. He wanted to plot his revenge, so he went to the village and killed someone and everyone bowed to him...

Samuel Hawksworth (11)
Ridgeway Middle School, Redditch

The Boy That Didn't Ask

Once upon a time there was a boy called Robin. One day Robin was bored so he went outside to play in the trees but he didn't ask permission. He was playing on the trees but then a strange lion walked up to him and said, 'Hello, do you want to get in my sack? It's full of candy.'
Robin believed him. He jumped in. The lion tied the sack – he was kidnapping him. When the lion wasn't looking Robin jumped out and ran home. He told his mom, she called the police, the lion was arrested.

Abbie Porter (11)
Ridgeway Middle School, Redditch

The Poor Old Goat

Once upon a time, in a valley far, far away, lived a goat, a lion, a bear and a wolf. They were all best friends, although the goat was left out. The lion, bear and wolf always made fun of the goat, just because of her looks. However, one day the goat came outside and knocked on the door of the wolf. The wolf said, 'Go away!'
She knocked on the lion's door, he said, 'Go away!'
Finally, she knocked on the bear's door and he gave her a big hug. They lived happily ever after.

Ethan Clements (11)
Ridgeway Middle School, Redditch

Recycleman

Recycleman said to Dobby, 'I am going to fly to Africa, New Zealand and France to pick up litter from nasty Litterman, and then I am going to the rest of the world to pick up litter.' Then when he was flying over Brazil he saw Litterman littering crisp packets and cans. When he flew down to catch him in the exact place, he had disappeared. Recycleman was surprised. He looked all over Rio de Janeiro then he saw Litterman flying in the clouds and Recycleman shot off quickly, caught Litterman and saved the day!

George Henry Sallis (8)
St Andrew's CE Primary School, Stafford

New Zealand

In New Zealand Jake and Sophie went to a volcano. Jake and Sophie were sprinting as fast as they possibly could but they just ran away from the volcano in time. There was one question – where would they live? So they went to British Airways and drove to Birmingham and home again. Back at home they were very excited. The flight was very fun because they flew to the other side of the world and back. They really enjoyed it. I guess it was extremely fun. It was rather fun because it was their first trip.

Robert Heynes (7)
St Andrew's CE Primary School, Stafford

In The Ocean

Once upon a time there lived a terrified mermaid called Milly and she lived in a cave. It was a very dark cave. Also a storm was coming in. She never came out of the cave because she was shy. A little fish swam into the dark spooky cave. He was called Billy. The cave was freaky. The fish could not see a thing. The fish found the mermaid. 'Can you be my friend?' said the fish.
'I don't know, I am scared of the nets that come down into the water.'
'Do not be frightened, I am with you!'

Chloe Hassall (7)
St Andrew's CE Primary School, Stafford

The Battle Of The Century

Once upon a time, in China, there were men called Will, Joe and George. Joe and George were baddies and they robbed everything valuable like gold and gems. Will was a judo master who wanted to stop the baddies from stealing. He trained many strong people in judo to help him defeat Joe and George. The baddies were also training strong people to steal from them.
100 days later the goodies and the baddies met and had a chilling fight. The goodies won and returned the gems to their gobsmacked owners. The goodies lived happily ever after.

Will Brumwell (8)
St Andrew's CE Primary School, Stafford

The Lost Ruby

Once upon a time lived a mermaid fairy called Twiler. Twiler was a nice girl. One day Twiler lost her ruby. It was special. Twiler went on an adventure to find her ruby. Twiler knew Jack Frost stole her ruby. Twiler cried to someone, 'What's your name?'
She answered, 'My name's Rebecca.'
Twiler said, 'Well hello Rebecca, please can you help? I know Jack Frost has my ruby. It's special to me, I've had it since I was little. Please.'
'OK,' said Rebecca. Rebecca hunted and found Jack Frost and returned the ruby.
'Oh thank you very much Rebecca!'

Dion Rogerson (8)
St Andrew's CE Primary School, Stafford

Thunderbirds' First Rescue

One day Jeff was working on Thunderbird Three. John called from space, 'Somebody's broken into the bank of London.'
'Come on Virgil, Thunderbirds are go!' bellowed Jeff.
They shot into Thunderbirds Two and Three. Off they went to London in their high speed jets.
Suddenly another ship came and a pilot opened the window. 'Who are you?' asked Virgil.
'You can call me The Hood and I've stolen the bank of London,' The Hood chuckled.
'I'm calling the police and taking you to jail.'
Quickly he was taken to prison and never seen again. Hooray for Thunderbirds.

Enys Lloyd (8)
St Andrew's CE Primary School, Stafford

The Mysterious Man

Once upon a time me and Lissy were playing in our bedroom. Someone burst into the room but before Lissy could say anything she was stuffed into a bag. I ran to the window but by that time Lissy had vanished.

The next day I stayed in my bedroom looking at a photo of me and Lissy at the beach. Just then a red light interrupted me. I followed it, hoping it would lead me to my sister, it did but she was in a cellar. The next minute a shadow popped out of the darkness holding Lissy's body...

Ella Marie Wells (8)
St Andrew's CE Primary School, Stafford

The Boy Cried Super Bob

Once upon a time lived a superhero called Super Bob. His power was flying. One day a boy called Paul called Super Bob to help him with the heavy wood.

The next day Paul wanted help again with something heavy. It was coal. When Super Bob got home he was tired and fell asleep. Then something bad happened! Paul saw a tiger, he was scared. He called Bob, nobody answered. Bob was asleep. Then Paul got eaten. Red blood was everywhere. Bob woke up, the phone was still ringing. Down the phone Super Bob heard Paul was sad.

Joseph Evans (8)
St Andrew's CE Primary School, Stafford

A Day In The Life Of The World With One Boy!

I woke up this morning and no one was there. Downstairs I turned on the news. No one was on air. Later I decided to take a trip to the sweet shop, but it was closed. Maybe they had changed their opening times. At home, on the journey to the couch, the calendar caught my eye. I was meant to be meeting my friends, now! I grabbed my coat and ran! I waited and waited but nothing. Back at home I drowned my sorrows in football television. I lay in bed thinking what a weird day it was, then slept!

Megan Elizabeth Ruskin Upright (10)
St Dominic's Priory School, Stone

Up, Up, And Away!

'What's this?' Saffron, Sam and Sienna pulled out an old carpet with bright patterns. On the news they saw Sandypaws was missing. They sat on the carpet and before they could blink it was flying. They agreed to use the carpet to find the puppy on Snowdon. They filled Sienna's backpack with snacks. It was cold and shivery on Snowdon. 'Sandypaws!' called Saffron. After ages searching Sam finally spotted Sandypaws. They held his collar so he wouldn't fall off the carpet. Back home Sienna noticed her backpack had been left behind. Well at least they still had the amazing carpet!

Miren Stacey (10)
St Dominic's Priory School, Stone

Untitled

Jason was adventurous, yet wayward. He was always getting himself into trouble, but this was by far the worst. He had tailed two men to an abandoned warehouse to meet his doom. The door slammed shut behind him. Dwelling in utter darkness. He was tricked. His heartbeat raced up to an unbelievable speed. Then out of the blue a blood-curdling shriek staggered his ears. Jason's instincts yelped to get out. He sprinted to the door, tugged. Locked. Jason glanced behind him. What was it? He had an idea, then smirked... Jason climbed out the window! He was free!

Jude Kent (9)
St Dominic's Priory School, Stone

Untitled

Have you ever had a dream? Well three young girls have: Esme, Georgina, Tabby and Conker the sausage dog AKA Chocolate Log. They all have a passion for, and a belief in, time travel, but everyone doubted them. The girls thought they were very good at inventing, they had been working on a time travel machine since finding a secret mechanical design plan at an antique fayre. At last it was finished and the girls were planning their adventure. The moon was full, the stars were shining. It was perfect. They were off. It was all fine until suddenly...

Tabitha Owen (9)
St Dominic's Priory School, Stone

The Dinosaur Adventure

One day two girls called Amanda and Tabby went to their time machine. It was the middle of the night. They pressed some buttons and they ended up in a lush green forest. Then they saw a dinosaur and they were happy. Amanda and Tabby went to a cave and right outside Tabby found a fossil of a tooth. They dug and dug until they had uncovered the entire skeleton, so they took a picture of the fossil and went back to the time machine. They went back to 2015.
The next day they went to the museum happily.

Amanda Ware (8)
St Dominic's Priory School, Stone

The Haunted House

Nothing moved in the dead of the night. The moon looked square from a distance. Daniel crept up the crumbling stairs and opened one of the huge wooden doors which creaked as he pushed.
Ahead of Daniel was a dusty, red carpeted spiral staircase. Daniel nervously walked up.
'Hello,' squeaked a miserable voice. Daniel screamed. At the top was a young girl called Emily.
'Hello,' replied Daniel, shivering with fear. Behind Emily was a plump, purple ghost. 'Argh!' bellowed Daniel.
'What?' questioned Emily.
'There's a ghost,' Daniel said trembling.
Emily screamed, 'Run!' They zoomed away. 'Thank you,' whispered Emily with delight.

Harriet Stubbs (9)
St Dominic's Priory School, Stone

Danger In The Palace

Sophisticated people whispering about him. He looked up, there she was, an immaculate woman with perfectly manicured nails. She picked up a zesty lemon cupcake with butter cream icing.
'No don't! It's poisonous! There is a French traitor amongst us,' he shouted breathlessly.
The queen immediately looked up to find a wrinkled bleeding man, 'What in the gracious world is happening?' she demanded.
'I'm here, just a humble man to help protect your majesty, the French are currently waiting for you to fall,' he spoke as if his words were from the heart.
'I can't believe this is happening again...'

Kyra Kaur (9)
St Dominic's Priory School, Stone

A Spacebowl Adventure

Excitedly I waited in the queue of the spacebowl ride with my best friend Daisy. Approaching the front my nerves grew. Soon it was Daisy's turn, finally mine. I was shaking as I looked over the dark tunnel entrance at the swirly whirlpool UFO and Plungepool below. I pushed off, the speed built quickly. I entered the whirlpool like a bullet spinning round and round. Eventually, I dropped through the hole at the bottom. Unexpectedly, my feet hit hard ground. I was in a hot mountainous world with stars shooting above my head. I heard Daisy whisper, 'Where are we?'

Sophie Victoria Titley (9)
St Dominic's Priory School, Stone

The Future

Hi, I'm Poppy, I'm thirteen years old. I think the future's boring. I was hoping for something better; flying cars and buses aren't exciting to me. People choose how much longer I live for. That's what I don't like about the future. The shortest life is one second, the longest life is 250 years. I will receive a letter in five weeks telling me how much longer I will live for. I am going to be tested today. I feel very nervous. I do hope I will pass...
I broke the record! I'll live for 570 more years!

Georgina Owen (10)
St Dominic's Priory School, Stone

The Dinosaur's Park

Owen and his two boys, James, who was 13, and his younger brother Charlie, went to see the newly built dinosaur park! 'Dad,' said Charlie, 'this is amazing.' They saw a big vast futuristic dinosaur park. They went and explored. Two hours later they were watching the eggs hatch. Suddenly the sirens went off. A loud booming voice said, 'Evacuate to main reception,' so they all evacuated but something terrible happened, the dinosaurs had escaped. Luckily Owen was in the army so he went out and returned them to their cages.

Hugo Caine (9)
St Dominic's Priory School, Stone

Untitled

High above the clouds it's 3015. Miny Marvel Island floated, life was happy, just like any ordinary country.
Suddenly Ultron the evil robot attacked Miny Marvel. 'I am Ultron the powerful undefeated mecanoid.' His threatening red eyes blinking in the moonlight. 'I want your floating island.' Ultron launched his fireball, knocking Iron Man out. Hulk tried to rescue Iron Man, Ultron fired his chest laser at Hulk. Hulk crossed his bulky green fists to block the laserbeam. Thor, with all his power, launched lightning. Ultron fell to the ground. The Miny Marvels surrounded him. Ultron flew away. 'I will defeat you!'

William Bennett (9)
St Dominic's Priory School, Stone

Untitled

Hi, I am Lucy and I am eleven years old. I have an older brother called Josh and he is seventeen. One day I saw a bright pink notebook with my name on the front cover. All of a sudden a gust of wind made all of the curtains shake. Out of the blue a green slimy blob let out a gigantic roar. Then, all of a sudden we all let out a scream so loud that I woke my idle brother...

Keighley Davies (11)
St Dominic's Priory School, Stone

The Pacific

Freedom! As lovely as it is, it creeps up on you and... complete darkness. You get used to your surroundings after a while. You spring up to the surface to take a quick breather. The ripples glide around you as if they're alive. I would go back down into the creek. The pebbles brush up against my scales. At first it is quite ticklish but then it can cut you at the very end. I settle in the slimy sand all alone and in the current. What? Argh! You must be thinking, how am I still talking?...

Philippa Ford (10)
St Dominic's Priory School, Stone

Dear Diary

Today, I woke up at six-thirty so I could have my favourite cereal before Louise, my sister. After I plodded upstairs I trod on a piece of Lego! School was modest because we got to paint our chair in art so we knew which was ours. Next English and double RE which was pretty jolly good. Lunch was horrid. After school was detention. Luckily, I wasn't on the list. When I got home I forgot to feed my dog. Suddenly, Dad burst though the door and exclaimed he was promoted. Dinner was okay. So nine out of ten.

Dylan Cunningham (10)
St Dominic's Priory School, Stone

Captain Cool

Dear Diary, today I was called out for duty and I saved a cat from a tree. As I was flying home I saw a poster saying: 'Captain Cool's our no. 1 hero!' But instead of my wacky T-shirt, out of the poster came a blue suit with an iceberg sign, a yellow belt and red gloves. I froze for a moment. Then I dashed home and neatly stitched the extraordinary suit bit by bit. Then I rushed out, followed by the alarm. More disaster had struck downtown. Then I became Captain Cool.

Edward Talbot (10)
St Dominic's Priory School, Stone

Street Child

Hi, my name is Jay. When I was three I was put in an old crumbly orphanage, I didn't like it there. So I ran away. In the middle of the night, I awoke with sweat dripping down my face, I had heard a bang, something had happened outside. I climbed from beneath the bin bags and opened the door. Cautiously, I stepped outside, in front of me I saw that a car had collided with another and it was dangerously near my hut. I had to move. Desperately I looked for somewhere to go, I really needed a miracle...

Evie Barlow (9)
St Elizabeth's RC Primary School, Tamworth

Robot Disaster!

In the middle of a city a clever scientist, who was very old, liked making robots. Once he made a robot that when he turned it on it ate him up! Angrily the robot ate everything in its way to the wall and broke through the wall. The huge robot ate everything in its way. Later a boy called Will saw everything so he made a robot that carried a bomb. Will threw the robot outside for the terrifying robot to eat. When the robot ate the robot the robot broke! The robot was recycled.

Vilmos Bogdanyi (9)
St Elizabeth's RC Primary School, Tamworth

The Brave Assassin

Faraway from the base, a cool, talented assassin called Connor was chasing a sloppy, smooth alien called Xaxar. At the base, the assassin had traps and he pulled out a knife and threw it at a rope and a rock fell down. So Xaxar went another way and got to the controls and launched a nuclear missile. Suddenly, the assassin appeared and reset the coordinates to the sun and the missile blew up and turned to ashes. He put Xaxar in a rocket and sent him to his planet. Everyone was celebrating that the assassin saved every person.

Callum Joshua Sleet (9)
St Elizabeth's RC Primary School, Tamworth

The Heroic Deed

In the fair town on Spring Lock there was a knight called Kodie and a dragon named Draco. One dark day, the kingdom's power source, Kingdom Sceptre, had gone missing. With their heads up high, Kodie and Draco volunteered to find the sceptre. Suddenly as they walked into a cave and retrieved the sceptre an earthquake occurred. Heroically, Draco used the power he had left and sealed his heart, soul and mind into the sceptre to save his best friend and a whole kingdom. Just as the sceptre was returned, so was Draco's spirit and that was the heroic deed!

Ryan Huntley (9)
St Elizabeth's RC Primary School, Tamworth

The Skeleton And Me

I didn't like it, my dad had gone. I was terrified! At that second, I felt a bony hand. As my vision changed, a skeleton hand touched the top of my tired head. I opened the door while running and screaming. I found myself at a dead end. My heart was pounding, my body was shivering. I didn't know what to do. I have never had an experience like this. Why now? The day Dad had gone... 'Please, I am young.' Then I heard a bang! My little brother tripped over his skeleton costume. I hate Halloween!

Sasha Pailing (8)
St James CE Primary School, Rugeley

ONCE UPON A TIME - **Staffordshire & Worcestershire**

Milly And The Little Fish

One beautiful sunny day, the little fish went for a short swim. All of a sudden a jellyfish saw him. He chased the little fish onto the island. 'Help! Help! I can't breathe!' shouted the little fish. A little girl heard his loud cry. Her name was Milly, all fish could hear her. She whistled. The little fish heard her impressive whistle and believed in himself. With all his courage he held his breath and bravely dived into the crystal-blue water. He was safe again in his house.

Hannah Hodgkiss (8)
St James CE Primary School, Rugeley

Jurassic Island

'Jurassic Island, Jurassic Island!' the fans chanted as the boat took them to Isla Nubla. But when the boat got there, there was screaming and shouting because everyone was running away from the T-rex, Indominus rex, raptors and Utar raptors because they'd escaped. In the middle of the commotion was dinosaur specialist James Mcraden, trying to calm down the Utar raptors and raptors. Finally, James was able to get the Utar raptors and raptors under control and find his partner Clair Darling. It was the ultimate battle between the Utar raptors and raptors Vs Indominus rex and the tyrannosaurus rex...

Millun Hazell (9)
St James CE Primary School, Rugeley

The Footballing Dog

Yesterday my dog Dan was playing in the back garden when suddenly he got struck by lightning! Next, Dan stopped what he was doing, got his ball and started doing football tricks. The next day, a boy was looking out of his window and spotted the dog doing tricks. Quickly he got on his bike, rode to the news and told them about the dog. And within two days the dog was known worldwide and was famous.

Thomas Larkin (9)
St James CE Primary School, Rugeley

The Helpful Robot

Once there was a girl who loved climbing cliffs, but she kept slipping and landing on her belly! Everyone laughed, all except the girl. One day she was walking in a forest and saw a robot who said, 'Hello, do you need help?'
'Yes, I do!' And she explained her problem.
He looked at her shoes and laughed. 'You need to clean your shoes with shoe polish instead of slime so you won't slip!'
So she did and nobody laughed anymore because she didn't slip again and she became the best climber in the world thanks to the helpful robot!

Amelia Long (7)
St James CE Primary School, Rugeley

The Ghosts Of The Trenches

In the war there were two men, one called Bob and one called Jeff.
Bob had been shot in the heart and Jeff had been beheaded.
A few days later a man called Bill saw the two ghosts and thought
if he was to catch them he would be paid loads of money. So the
very next day he called the ghost hunter. When they got there they
set up camp.
Three days later the ghost hunters got back to Bill and said they
had got them.

Matthew Taylor (8)
St James CE Primary School, Rugeley

The Awakening

There was once a man who loved to explore. On an ordinary day
he found an unexplored graveyard, he had to go in because his
curiosity got the better of him and he walked in. Suddenly there
was a huge rumble and a bony hand popped up out of the ground.
While he was watching, hands popped up, finally a grave rumbled
and out came a transparent figure! All he heard was a great moan
and a ghostly voice said, 'We are coming.' What was happening?
Ghouls? Ghosts? Or zombies? Should I tell you the tale? Maybe
another day...

Jacob Fox-Bailey (8)
St James CE Primary School, Rugeley

The Phantom Footballer

There lived a phantom but he wasn't any old phantom, he was the almighty phantom footballer. On the 12/11/05, the grand FA Cup Final was on, Manchester United were playing the champions Manchester City. It was neck and neck in the final. Ten minutes until Clichy fouled Rooney in the box, it was a penalty to Manchester United. All of a sudden the ball went missing, everybody wondered who had taken the ball. Then all of a sudden they heard a laugh in the air, it was the phantom footballer...

Louis Jay Cope (9)
St James CE Primary School, Rugeley

The Princess And The Strange Girl

I am in my room smacking my head against the pillow, my mum is calling me so I get dressed into a summer dress decorated with flowers and suns. Today it is at least fifty degrees. I have my breakfast and go to school. When I get to English class I see a girl, a strange girl. *Who could she be?* I think. Maths now. There she is again. At break I spy on her because she is in the school garden. I can't believe my eyes.

Lucie Haines (8)
St James CE Primary School, Rugeley

I Have Invented A Planet Full Of Bunnies

There was a little girl named Allison. She had invented a planet full of bunnies. She kept on thinking if it would come true. Then in about one minute it came true. She went to space, and when she got there she made a friend named Baba. It was a bunny. So Allison and Baba were very close, wherever they went they always included each other. They loved each other forever.

Hannah Smith (7)
St James CE Primary School, Rugeley

Town Wars

Just that day, someone new joined Elmor. Bob hated what he was seeing! Bob did not approve, he also saw what everyone was fighting for, a dog that said Jake on its collar. He sprinted for it but Java the opposite town got it. He charged but he was not looking where he was going and he dropped the fluffy dog. Gumball caught it but he stepped on his tail and fell onto Bob. Bob caught it but he held it a little hard and it went *ping!* It was a robot!

Amy Edwards (9)
St James CE Primary School, Rugeley

Enchanted Alicorn

Hannah and Alice saw a blinding light. The light came from the middle of the trees. Just then, Hannah heard some footsteps. She looked behind her, amazed. She saw an alicorn! Then the alicorn neighed, it let Hannah and Alice on its back and then they whooshed away. This was just the start of their amazing adventure. They flew all the way around the world on the alicorn's back, having loads more amazing adventures, and meeting loads more magic animals every day.

Pippa Rowles (8)
St James CE Primary School, Rugeley

Ella And Me

Right there at that moment Alice saw that her wish had come true, her new fairy friend named Ella was a miracle. But Sheler was hiding behind a stone rock, and once she had found out what Alice's secret was she fled to tell the entire school. Sheler told everyone the whole story of Alice's secret friend Ella. As soon as Alice had heard what happened, she was devastated. Suddenly Sheler came and gasped because Alice had told everyone about Sheler. Sheler was furious, but the head teacher was very cross with Sheler and Alice was popular yet again.

Bo Eleanor Spears (9)
St James CE Primary School, Rugeley

Superheroes Save The Day

In the heat of New York City, Fire Freda, Triumphant Trixie, Amazing Elody and Own Way Oly were chilling in the fire tower. Then Dr Light and Jurassic Jim went to destroy the city. Amazing Elody froze Dr Light and Jim, and Triumphant Trixi told them that they were absolutely rubbish, but then the ice melted. Dr Light and Jim ran off. Trixie, Freda and Elody noticed that Own Way Oly was still at home. They raced back. Own Way Oly got Dr Light and Jim into a net and all was well.

Lizzy Dewsbury (7)
St James CE Primary School, Rugeley

The Magic Book

Once, a group of geeks joined a new college. Perrie liked a boy called Chris. Chris waved at the group but a mean girl pushed them out the way and hugged Chris. Leigh-Ann mumbled, 'Let's go to the library!' Jade went to pick a book. An old leather book fell on her head. Jesy noticed the book. She raced and they took it back to the dorm. During free period the girls sat in a circle with the book in the middle.

The next morning they were like hot pop super stars with teen magical sparkling spells that do anything.

Danielle Rotchell (8)
Yarlet School, Stafford

The Adventure To Atlantis

One dark evening, SpongeBob opened a letter with a map in it. It said, 'Map to Atlantis.' SpongeBob quickly jumped on Patrick who was peacefully sleeping on the couch. He woke up in a fuss and he yawned, 'What is it?'
SpongeBob shouted back, 'We have got a map to Atlantis.' They drove off. Finally they found a sign that looked like a piranha pointing into a mouthlike cave. Patrick was scared of the cave. They drove on to Atlantis but they came across a hole in the ground. They were going too fast...!

Joseph Thorpe (8)
Yarlet School, Stafford

The Cricket Match

Once, when the England team were warming up, their opposition New Zealand came on. England were nervous but determined. They were at Lords on a dry day. The captain Alistair Cook was encouraging them. It was the match. England won the toss and chose to field. After the first five it was 25-5. England were on track. After the 20 overs they were all out for 75. England had a great fight and played well and took runs. Moen Ali and Joe Root hit a great partnership of 20 runs. But Josh Butler soon hit a six to win.

Jamie Betteley (9)
Yarlet School, Stafford

The Spies Who Fight

Once there were two spies called Dan and Lauren, they were part of a spy group called MI6, who tried to save the country. Dan drove an Aston Martin DB9. He had a Russian girlfriend called Lauren. They suddenly heard some news. Goldfinger was in town... Quickly they climbed into the Aston and raced to the city. The city had lots of tall buildings like the Shard and the Gherkin. Suddenly an alarm went off inside the Shard! Lauren pulled Dan towards a dark and gloomy room. Someone jumped out. It was Goldfinger! 'So, we meet again Mr Bond!'

Henry Pickering (8)
Yarlet School, Stafford

Radical Robots

Once upon a time lived three rich gentlemen. They were obnoxious men who didn't like giving any of their money away. Noah was a skillful man. Tom was very tall and Lucas was slim. They all sold cars together. In the richest town in the world lived two robots, Lucy who was high tech and Sam who was lovely. They planned to steal the rarest car in the world. At twelve midnight they arrived at the car show room. They headed towards the car of their dreams. Suddenly the car popped up, it was a fake. Noah, Tom and Lucas laughed.

Noah Beeston (9)
Yarlet School, Stafford

YOUNG WRITERS
INFORMATION

We hope you have enjoyed reading this book – and
that you will continue to in the coming years.

If you're a young writer who enjoys reading and creative
writing, or the parent of an enthusiastic poet or story
writer, do visit our website
www.youngwriters.co.uk. Here you will find free
competitions, workshops and games, as well as
recommended reads, a poetry glossary and our blog.

If you would like to order further copies of
this book, or any of our other titles, give us a
call or visit **www.youngwriters.co.uk.**

Young Writers, Remus House
Coltsfoot Drive, Peterborough, PE2 9BF

(01733) 890066 / 898110
info@youngwriters.co.uk